EDMUND+OCTAVIA

THE DULCIE CHAMBERS MUSEUM MYSTERIES

by Kerry J Charles

THE
FRAGILE
FLOWER

A Dulcie Chambers Museum Mystery

Kerry J Charles

EDMUND+OCTAVIA

Cover Image: *#4 White Convolvulus*, 1876, Charlotte Anna Lefroy. This image is in the public domain.

ISBN: 0989457664
ISBN-13: 978-0-9894576-6-8

Edmund+Octavia, Falmouth, Maine, USA

This book is dedicated
to those who took the chance
with a leap of faith.

CONTENTS

*I found I could say things
with color and shapes
that I couldn't say any other way
- things I had no words for.*
~ Georgia O'Keeffe

CHAPTER ONE

"They call it *Young Man's Death*."

The voice slid softly down the back of Dulcie's neck. It wasn't a whisper or a murmur, but the gentle melodious voice of a woman who had lived in Bermuda for a lifetime. Dulcie turned slowly and smiled. "Do you know why?"

The woman laughed, a beautiful, low sound like the turquoise waves rushing against the shore nearby. "It is a name from the old country. My grandmother was English. I visited her in Cornwall when I was a very little girl. Once, I picked this flower," she gestured toward the painting on the wall behind Dulcie. "My grandmother, she gasped and said, 'Cassandra, do you have a boyfriend? Because if you do, he is in big trouble now!' Of course then I made her explain it all. They say that if a girl picks this flower, her lover will die."

1

"Did you believe it?" Dulcie asked.

The woman shook her head gently. "Of course not! First, I did not have a boyfriend. Second, I was born too practical, an old woman even at a young age. I had no time for nonsense. And third," the woman leaned closer to Dulcie and said *sotto voce*, "she was crazy as a bat!"

Dulcie burst out laughing. The sound rang in the otherwise silent room. She held out her hand. "I'm Dulcie Chambers. I'm here from the States."

The woman held out her hand as well, beautifully dark with a simple yet perfect sapphire and gold ring on it. She shook Dulcie's hand. "I am Cassandra Watts, a volunteer here at the Bermuda National Gallery. However, I believe that you are more than just *from the States* Ms. Chambers? You see, I've always kept up with my studies. Dr. Dulcinea Chambers is the director of the Maine Museum of Art. Would you be the same Dr. Chambers, or is this an amazing coincidence of mistaken identity?"

"You're right, I confess. No coincidence. I'm going a bit incognito at the moment as a quick break." Dulcie sighed, trying to put thoughts of her situation at home out of her mind. "As you must know, however, if this," she waved toward the paintings, "is in your blood, it's impossible to take even a quick break."

Cassandra smiled. "You are right. When I travel I must see the museums wherever I go. But tell me, does this exhibit interest you, or simply the museum in general?"

"I'll be diplomatic and say 'the museum' but between the two of us, I'm very interested in this exhibit. Botanicals have always fascinated me. I think it's the cross between science and art, and possibly even a bit of historical witchcraft thrown in for good measure." Dulcie looked back at the painting on the wall. *Convolvulus.* Morning glory. She had seen variations of them so many times growing wild back in Maine.

Cassandra looked over at the painting as well. "Yes, the balms and teas of herbal healers long ago. I think that with all of our pills and shots today, we have lost the effect of a good healing." Her blue eyes were the same color as her ring and sparkled equally as much. Dulcie could imagine Cassandra living centuries earlier, mixing potions and healing people with 'mystical powers.' As if reading Dulcie's mind, Cassandra leaned toward her and whispered, "My Aunties told me that I have witches in my ancestry!"

Dulcie's eyes were wide. "Do you think that's true?" she asked.

Cassandra shrugged her shoulders. "First one must believe in witchcraft. As for me, I believe in science," she smiled, then nodded toward the paintings, "and art."

Dulcie understood. Art. It was her salvation. The constant in a life that kept changing. She could always find herself again, stay centered in the confusion, when she walked into a museum and simply wandered through the quiet galleries. Sometimes she wondered if it was that feeling, more than any interest in history or the artwork itself, that drew her to the career she had chosen. She pulled herself from her thoughts realizing that Cassandra was speaking again.

"The artist here was a woman. I find that interesting. Lady Charlotte Anna LeFroy. Her husband was the Governor of Bermuda in the 1870s, and a scientist. She must have enjoyed science too, as these works are only a few of her botanicals. She did many paintings in Tasmania where they also lived. India as well, where she travelled with her first husband." Cassandra turned to Dulcie. "Don't you find it unfortunate that women of the past often led such exciting lives, yet it is the men that we hear stories of? We know little of Lady LeFroy. We must try to learn about her from her work."

Dulcie nodded in agreement. The morning glory vines curled and spiraled around each other like miniature corkscrews. They were so delicate. Dulcie could imagine Lady LeFroy concentrating hard, pushing aside the rest of the world, and using a tiny brush to create them. She would have been completely focused on her work, oblivious to anything happening around her.

That's what Dulcie wanted to do right now. Tune out everything else but her work. She turned to Cassandra. "I'm considering an exhibit of botanicals from around the world for my museum," she said. "I'm glad to find an example of a woman artist that I might be able to include."

Cassandra smiled. "As am I." She put her hand gently on Dulcie's arm. "You must let me know how you do with your work. I see great things in you Dr. Dulcinea." She squeezed Dulcie's arm gently as though she were a little child, then drifted off into the shadows of the next gallery.

Dulcie turned away from the final painting in the exhibit, pushed through the heavy glass doors and stepped lightly down the carpeted stairs. She emerged onto the wide stone steps that fronted the building. Squinting in the bright light, she searched through her bag for her sunglasses. Only after a few moments of rummaging did she realize that they were still on top of her head.

She slid them down then looked around, trying to decide what to do next. This trip to Bermuda had been a lark. No, it was actually an escape. Her cell phone had at least five unread text messages. Fortunately they had stopped once she left the US since she didn't have international calling access. She did have email, however, and did not even want to check that.

Dulcie slowly descended the imposing steps. The late afternoon shadows were beginning to encroach on the street. Carefully looking in both directions several times — Bermuda traffic came from the opposite direction from what she normally expected — she crossed and made her way to the waterfront.

A ferry blasted its horn as it pulled away from the dock. She watched it for several minutes as it went across the harbor toward Salt Kettle. '*Dan would love it here*,' she thought. Her brother was back in Maine running his business of giving tours around Casco Bay on the small yacht that he and Dulcie had bought. Dulcie could imagine him doing the same thing in Hamilton Harbor.

Bermuda was the closest place that she could think of where she could truly run away. Nova Scotia had been a possibility, but geographically it seemed too much like Maine for her. The flight to Bermuda from Boston had been under two hours, but when she arrived she felt as though she was half way around the world. The water was a brilliant aqua. The houses, painted soft pastel colors with white roofs, looked like cakes with fondant icing. To her ear everyone spoke with a gentle accent, somewhere between British and a Caribbean lilt. She had laughed to herself thinking how flat and ugly her voice must sound to them.

Her passport was due to expire in a few months. A moment of panic had set in after she bought the nonrefundable ticket, but had forgotten to check her passport's date. She had just made it in to the country under the pesky six-month rule. She had to remember to renew, just in case she needed to escape again.

There it was once more, that word: escape. Why did she need to escape? There really was nothing to escape from. She had never had a relationship with him. They had never really even been on a date. There was the one "thank you" dinner, but that was all. Yet she felt betrayed. Why?

Deep down, she knew why. Even though they had not been intimate by the usual definition, the fact that they worked together on two separate murder cases threw them together in a very intimate way. Dulcie tried to convince herself that they were simply working too closely. However, she could not deny that he had seemed to show more of an interest in her than was strictly professional.

But then, the bombshell. He was unavailable. Completely unavailable. He must have known it would affect her, or he would have mentioned it from the start. He must have known it *did* affect her, or he would not have seen any need to leave multiple text messages.

She was not going to let it bother her any more, however. She shook her head vigorously and walked on down the street. Nicholas Black would continue on the path of his life, and she would continue on hers. And hopefully those paths would not cross again.

 C3

Nicholas Black sat back in the uncomfortable wooden chair and looked around the conference room of the law offices that his grandfather had founded. He had just finished signing papers. The lawyer handling his case, the droning Robert Cavanaugh, Esquire, walked in the room as Nick put down the pen. "Ah, good. Perfect timing," he said in a nasally voice with pudgy lips that barely moved. "She'll contest again probably, but this time she can't stall any longer. We've got her." He tapped Nick's laptop with the eraser end of his pencil. The computer contained the critical piece of evidence, grounds for divorce that were irrefutable: adultery.

The first time that Nick had asked for a divorce, just after he had finished law school, she had laughed at him. The issue was money, of course. It had always been money. That's why she had married him in the first place, although he had been completely unaware of the fact. Stupid of him, in retrospect. They had known each other since childhood, yet she had never shown any particular interest in him then.

She had managed to stall the divorce proceedings on several occasions. Not content with a standard alimony payment, she was simply holding out for more money. She knew that when he reached the age of thirty, only several months away at this point, he would receive a huge trust fund. If they divorced before then, she would get none of it. But by dragging everything on until his birthday, she would then be entitled to half. Prolonging everything had little impact on her life other than requiring her to maintain a low profile. It was all lawyers' work.

Why had Nick married her? He sighed as Robert Cavanaugh, Esquire shuffled through the papers. Nick knew why. He was young. He was easily manipulated.

He let his family rule his life. She was beautiful of course, which always affects the situation, especially for a relatively inexperienced college boy. She had also done everything in her power to entice him. That is, until the day after the wedding, which had taken place the day after his graduation from Harvard. That's when it all began to change.

Nick had not recognized it immediately, but their 'similar interests' quickly began to fade away. He had always enjoyed museums. She now found them boring. He liked to sail. She suddenly hated how the wind snarled up her hair. He liked to go to his family's quiet beach house and spend the evenings reading a good book. She now preferred to stay in Boston and go out at night with her friends.

When he mentioned his troubles to his parents, their response was decisive. "Make it work. Besides," his father had said, "when you become a lawyer and join the firm, she'll be an asset." Nick didn't want an asset. He wanted a friend. He wanted a companion. He wanted a wife.

He had been in law school for two years and was facing the bar exam. He had taken to closing the door of his study for hours so that he could review for it. In fact, he had not been studying. He had been doing nothing but stare at the walls and wonder how to get out of the mess that his life had become. As the day of the exam drew nearer, he knew that he was not ready. He also knew that he had never intended to take it in the first place.

His link to Robert Cavanaugh, Esquire had begun as a class project in law school. Nick had been researching a case and his father, now retired, had suggested Cavanaugh as a good source of information. Of course the younger lawyer could not refuse to help the son of a senior partner and grandson of the firm's founder.

The relationship between Cavanaugh and Nick could not exactly have been termed a friendship. It was more of a mutual understanding. Cavanaugh was many things, but stupid was not one of them. He quickly realized that Nick's questions did not exactly pertain to the case that he was studying. Cavanaugh knew that they were of a more personal nature. He sympathized with the young law student. Robert Cavanaugh, Esquire had been used for his money too, and had also experienced some difficulty extricating himself from his own situation.

Now Cavanaugh looked across the table at Nick. "Yep, you've got her this time. And not a moment too soon as you're well aware." The final word hummed through his nose. "I'll get this through as fast as I can."

Nick nodded. He would have smiled, but he found no pleasure in any of it. He was tired, drained. "Thanks, Bob. You don't know how much I appreciate this. I know it's been tough, especially with my father not exactly supportive."

Cavanaugh waived his hand quickly over the table, as if to clear away the invisible dust in the air. "He's retired. The rest of us are in charge now. Besides, he doesn't know what it's like to get hosed. Or at least, I don't think he knows."

This time Nick did smile, although ruefully. "No, I don't think he does." His parents had always been on the same team, putting family honor and pride before anything else. He had heard many arguments behind closed doors, but before the rest of the world they were a united front. Personal happiness, individual happiness, was irrelevant.

Cavanaugh collected the papers together, tapped the edges on the table several times until they were perfectly aligned, then stood up. Nick did as well. He stuck out his hand and shook Cavanaugh's awkwardly.

"I'll let you know a court date. And it will be *well* before your birthday, you have my word," Robert Cavanaugh, Esquire squawked through his nose. With that, he held the door open for Nick, who walked through it for what would be, hopefully, the last time.

⍥

Dulcie returned to her room at the Hamilton Princess Hotel. She usually liked to stay somewhere near a beach so that she could swim, but this was a different sort of excursion. For this trip she just wanted to ride the ferry around the harbor, stare at the palm trees waving over the ocean, and of course visit the Bermuda National Gallery, an easy walk from the hotel.

Truth be told though, the biggest draw of the Hamilton Princess for her was high tea, to which Dulcie had happily succumbed the day before. When she was in Bermuda she had to restrain herself from having high tea every single day, which she could have, easily. '*Why don't we do this in America?*' she had thought once again while eyeing the three-tiered plate stand. The waiter had carefully described all of the little sandwiches and treats, but Dulcie could not remember a single one. It didn't matter. They were all so good. She'd attempted to appear ladylike as she devoured them all while sipping tea and reading a book.

Dulcie found herself smiling as she thought about that lovely hour devoted entirely to food and fiction.

Now, reality had come screaming back. She stood in the middle of her room and eyed her laptop as though it was the enemy.

She did not want to open it. There would be emails. Too many emails. And not just from him either. She reached beyond it on the table and picked up the bottle of wine that she'd grabbed at the duty free shop after her arrival. Bordeaux. A label that she usually didn't see in the States. She had spent too much on it and did not care. She had opened it the previous night, and it had not disappointed. Now she popped out the cork and searched around the room for a glass. Something that resembled a whiskey tumbler was in the bathroom with a little cardboard cover over it to ensure, somehow, that it was sparkling clean. Good enough.

She poured a glass of wine, took a deep breath, and opened her laptop. The messages began downloading. They kept downloading. Dulcie looked away, not wanting to see his name appear. She stood up and opened the door to the balcony.

With the gentle breeze fluttering the curtains, Dulcie at last turned to the computer. Oddly, there was only one message from Nicholas Black. It simply said:

Dulcie, I've been trying to get in touch via text. Just heard you were away. Hope all is well. I'd like to see you when you get back.   —Nick

That was it? She had expected more. Should she reply? She sat back and sipped her wine. Then she noticed the series of emails from Rachel.

Rachel had been Dulcie's assistant since Dulcie had become the director of the museum. Rachel had started out as a volunteer at the front desk but had proved her capabilities well. She had a way of being able to second-guess everything that Dulcie needed before she needed it. It was a natural fit, so when it was obvious that Dulcie needed an assistant, it was equally obvious who that person would be.

Now, however, it seemed that Rachel was in over her head. Dulcie started with the oldest message and worked her way up:

> *Visiting artist is here... not happy ... needs larger place, on ocean with north-facing studio ... must have room for wife and sister as well ... needs different brand of paint in museum studio, must order from France ... will only work with maximum of five students for master classes ... must have freshly brewed green tea from Ceylon...*

"Oh my!" Dulcie said out loud. She immediately wrote back:

> *Rachel, hang in there. I'll be back tomorrow and clear everything up. Sorry you're stuck with this situation. I had no idea! Thanks for all your work so far. —Dulcie*

Logan Dumbarton. Noted for his abstract oils of seascapes. At least, most art critics assumed they were seascapes, and Logan never denied it. His sister was his business manager and had initially contacted Dulcie with the idea for Logan to come as a visiting artist. The sister and Dulcie had emailed and telephoned over several months, and Dulcie had believed that all of the plans were in place, which was why she had left his initial arrival in Rachel's capable hands.

For one brief moment Dulcie thought about calling Rachel. Then she decided against it. She would be back soon enough and perhaps most of the issues would resolve themselves. Dulcie did find it strange that there were so many concerns, though. The sister, Linda, had seemed perfectly capable, professional and reasonable. Yet she had never indicated that she would be coming as well, and certainly had never mentioned that her brother was bringing his wife. Or that he even had a wife. '*That must be a new development*,' thought Dulcie. '*I'm losing my touch. I used to know all the gossip about the big names.*'

She closed the laptop, firmly deciding against any reply to Nick. She really didn't have anything to say.

No great artist ever
sees things as they really are.
If he did, he would cease
to be an artist.
~ Oscar Wilde

CHAPTER TWO

"After all of these years you *still* have no idea how to make a cup of tea! Are you a *complete* idiot?" Dulcie heard the low, snarling words from where she stood at the end of the hallway. She proceeded in the direction of the voice at a slow pace, letting her heels click loudly on the marble floor to announce her approach.

As Dulcie reached the room, Logan Dumbarton sat perfectly poised at his easel mixing paints with a small spatula while the person that Dulcie assumed was his sister scurried about in the corner with an electric kettle. She looked like an ever-efficient mouse. Her brownish-grayish-blondish stick-like hair was pulled back in a low, short ponytail with a rubber band. Dulcie wondered if she slept with it like that. It looked permanent.

Dulcie took several steps into the room and opened her mouth with what she intended to be a greeting, but what instead came out as a small gasp. She found herself staring at another woman who was a very stark contrast to the lady rattling teacups over in the corner. This woman's hair was also pulled back, but with what was obviously a Hermès scarf. The flowing locks cascading from it were thick, glossy, long and nearly black. Her dark eyes were rimmed softly with ebony liner so that they appeared almost luminous. Her petite frame was stretched across a royal-blue woolen blanket that contrasted with the glow of her golden skin, very evident given the fact that she was completely naked.

She wiggled on the blanket. "Logan, this itches!" she whined.

"Yes, my love. That is the price we must pay for immortality. I'm nearly done here. As soon as I get some proper tea we can take a break," he said in a gentle voice while shooting a venomous look in the direction of his sister. Dulcie waited for him to finish his stroke before she moved farther into the room.

"Good afternoon! I'm so sorry that I couldn't be here to meet you when you first arrived. I'm Dulcie Chambers," she held out her hand as she walked across the room.

Logan Dumbarton put down his brush deliberately. He eased himself off his stool with a hand theatrically placed on an aching back, then stood. He touched her fingertips with his, bringing her hand to his lips, and kissed the back of it.

"The pleasure is all mine," he said softly.

Dulcie was caught completely off guard. She looked at him with wide eyes for a moment, then found herself blinking rapidly as her senses returned.

"Logan, are we done?" the whining voice asked.

Dulcie turned to the vision now sitting up on the blanket, reaching for her robe.

"Yes, my love. I suppose we are for now." Logan Dumbarton turned again to Dulcie and said, "Allow me to introduce my wife, Isabel. And you've spoken with my sister, Linda, on several occasions I believe," he gestured across the room to the woman now dipping a tea bag into a mug of steaming water.

Dozens of thoughts and questions were now running through Dulcie's head. Who was this sister who had seemed so confident and proficient on the telephone? Where had this other woman come from who now was evidently Logan's wife? And why was he painting her nude when he was known for abstract seascapes? Dulcie blinked again and said, "I hope that you're settling in well. I understand that there were some concerns at first?"

"Ah, nothing that we couldn't solve. Linda takes care of everything so well." He smiled at his sister who now handed him the tea. Dulcie noticed that Linda did not return the smile.

"Would you like some tea?" Linda asked Dulcie in a flat voice.

Dulcie shook her head. "Thank you, but no. And I feel a bit awkward. I should be offering all of you tea since you are the guests here, not the other way around!"

"We feel so at home already," said Logan. "Don't even think of it!" He smiled with a very beautiful, pearly white expanse of teeth.

Dulcie reached toward Linda and shook her hand. "So nice to meet you at last although I feel as though we've already met, since we've been in touch for some time."

Linda nodded but said nothing. She forced a smile.

"Is that supposed to look like me?" Isabel had joined them, wrapped in a silk robe that gaped loosely. She jabbed a finger at the canvas.

Logan laughed. Dulcie thought it sounded a bit condescending. "My sweet, it's representational. You are the essence. The inspiration. The muse!" He patted her bottom and she squealed softly, giggling.

Dulcie felt as though she'd walked into someone's penthouse apartment. Worse, someone's bedroom. *"This is a museum! My museum!"* she reminded herself.

Logan continued, "Allow me to *properly* introduce this exquisite creature, my wife, Isabel."

The woman extended her hand limply and shook Dulcie's with as little effort as possible.

Dulcie spoke first before Logan could make any more saccharine, endearing comments. She was finding them difficult to stomach. "It's a pleasure to meet you, and I'm very glad that you could accompany your husband on this excursion." She quickly turned toward the canvas. "But I must confess that I share Isabel's confusion. Are you shifting your focus from seascapes now to the human form?"

Logan laughed again. The throaty chuckle that he seemed to emit prior to every utterance was getting on Dulcie's nerves. "I have decided to take this opportunity of working in a new venue to explore alternative directions. You see, by placing Isabel against the cerulean background, I am fusing an image of the sparkling sun and the waves with their boundless, sleek curves, into the deep blue essence of the mysterious depths."

Linda turned away. She busied herself writing in a notebook. Dulcie wished that she could do the same. She had heard many artists describe their work in self-flattering terms, but this took the proverbial cake.

"Well, I'm glad that you are inspired by being here. And we are indeed honored to have you. All of you." She turned slightly toward Linda. "I wanted to work out some of the details of the upcoming class when you have a few moments?" She looked back and forth between Logan and Linda, not certain who would respond.

Logan had already pulled Isabel onto his lap. Linda said, "I'll take care of that. Could we speak somewhere else, though? I'm somewhat allergic to turpentine — the odor makes me feel nauseous."

'*That's not the only thing,*' thought Dulcie. "Certainly," she said aloud. "Let's go to my office."

Linda quickly grabbed her bag. "I'll see you back at the house, Logan. Dinner will be ready by eight."

"Excellent," he replied flatly without looking at her. He was dabbing at the painting again with Isabel wiggling on his thigh.

Linda sat across from Dulcie in her office. Neither had spoken since they had left the studio. They looked at each other. Linda exhaled loudly and slowly. "I really need to apologize," she said, breaking the silence.

Dulcie began to object but Linda stopper her. "No, I must. You see, my brother does not mean to be difficult. He is so focused on his work. And his health has always been, well, I suppose *fragile* is the best word. He has his good days and bad. He works so much, you see, and it's very wearing."

'*Wearing for whom?*' Dulcie thought, but kept it to herself. Instead, she said, "I understand. But I do want to apologize to you for not having all of the accommodations in place. I just assumed that he would be with us for only a month at the most, and on his own."

"And that was the correct assumption. But again, Logan needed me with him. He didn't tell me until the night before he was scheduled to leave. He thought that I had been coming all along although I remember telling him that I would be staying in London to take care of business matters. He has an exhibition in September that's been a bear to plan."

"Forgive me if I sound rude, but I didn't realize that he had married," Dulcie said. She knew that she was being very direct, but the whole situation felt like it was becoming a circus. She had decided to give up on platitudes.

"Yes, that's new," Linda said as she slumped back in her chair. "Logan never seemed to be interested in women." She put up her hand as if to stop Dulcie's next words. "No, he wasn't interested in men either if that's what you're thinking." Dulcie was about to respond that she wasn't, but Linda didn't seem to notice. "He just didn't seem... interested. At all. In anyone. Then he went to a party at some photographer's loft in Chelsea, and saw Isabel. I wasn't there, but I heard that he kept staring at her. She was indifferent to him. Unimpressed. She must have known who he was. How could she not know? That must have been part of her charm, though. You see, everyone fawns over him. *The Great Artist.*" She said the last words with an edge of sarcasm. "He became obsessed with her and eventually convinced her to see him. From there it was only a few weeks before they were married."

"Truly a whirlwind," said Dulcie.

Linda did not hear her. She continued on in the same droning voice, "From that point on he's been with Isabel constantly. His *little muse*, he calls her. And no matter what plans I make, they change at the last minute." She stopped at last and sighed. Then, she looked across the desk at Dulcie as though she was surprised to see her sitting there. "Forgive me. I've been under a lot of pressure."

Dulcie nodded. She decided to refrain from speech until Linda was silent for at least a few moments.

Linda continued, more slowly, "You see, he really is fragile and that's what actually frightens me about this whole situation. He's been pushing himself in new directions artistically, not to mention staying up late with her. Little sleep, new work, not eating correctly, drinking more… I feel as though it's a disaster waiting to happen. I thought that Isabel would be staying in London at least for the first week or so that Logan was here in Maine, but of course that was not the case. That's why I felt that Logan was right to want me here as well. Someone to take care of all the little details. God knows Isabel could never do it." Linda stopped, and her focus shifted to Dulcie again.

Now Dulcie felt as though she could finally speak. "Of course. I understand, and you are all very welcome. You did find a place to stay that was suitable?"

"Yes, Rachel was a huge help there. It's in a town called Cape Elizabeth."

Dulcie thought, *I'm sure that's costing the museum a fortune!* Aloud she said, "Does it have the correct situation for Logan's personal studio?"

"Absolutely. I think that the studio would have been the second bedroom, but I'm very comfortable in a small space off the kitchen. I think it would have been the pantry – it's quite an old house. But I'm fine. I make all his meals and am typically up before him in the mornings, so no matter. It's actually quite helpful to be there, near the kitchen."

Dulcie wasn't convinced. She changed the subject. "Logan's master classes are scheduled to start this week. Will he be ready for them?" Linda seemed to think that Logan needed to be placated, but Dulcie was increasingly annoyed with the idea. He was a guest, yet he was also there to work. Not only was the museum giving him a stipend, Dulcie had also agreed to cover his expenses. These seemed to be increasing rapidly.

"Yes, I'll make sure that he is," said Linda.

"I understand that there was some concern about the number of students in the class?"

Linda looked away, suddenly embarrassed. "He said that he can handle only five. Any more would be very exhausting."

The Master Class in Abstract Painting with Logan Dumbarton had been advertised briefly and had received a great deal of interest. Although the fee for the course was steep by the museum's normal standards, seven people had signed up. The maximum that Linda had agreed upon originally had been ten. "We can close registration now, but we do have seven people already. They have all paid, so I feel that I can't deny them a spot at this point. Perhaps if I speak to Logan about this…"

"No, no! I'll handle it!" Linda looked flustered. "I'm sure it will be fine. I just don't want him to be overtaxed."

Something felt very odd about the entire situation. Dulcie tried to keep herself from being concerned but was having difficulty. She told herself that since this was the first master class that she had arranged at the museum, the kinks in the process were normal. The next time would go much more smoothly.

"If you think that will work best, then I'll leave it with you, Linda," said Dulcie. "The other point that we should talk about is the subject matter. The class description said that the students would be painting seascapes, including *plein air* sessions as weather permits. Logan seems to have gone in a new direction personally, but I hope that he can still honor our agreement and work with the students using his previous style."

Linda said nothing. Convincing Logan of anything was never easy. He always had excuses for everything that he did. Or, more accurately, everything that he did not do. Linda could hear it now: *my sinuses are hurting, the sun is giving me headaches, the fog destroys my canvas....* "I'll speak to him," was all that she said.

"Wonderful," said Dulcie, trying to keep the edge of sarcasm from her voice. "The first class will be on Thursday at 10 AM. That one is scheduled for the studio here at the museum, regardless of weather, since it's the introduction. And, because it's an introduction, it will only last for three hours. We're providing lunch for the students that day, but after that, they will be on their own for lunch each day. Is there anything specific that we can order in for Logan?"

Anything specific. Linda could tell her in extremely specific detail exactly what Logan would want. And as soon as it arrived, it would be incorrect. "I'll check with him," she replied.

Dulcie felt as though she was getting nowhere with the conversation. Masking her frustration she said, "Is there anything elsc that all of you might need at this point?"

Linda shook her head. "No. Not at this point. Thank you." She stood, even though Dulcie had not indicated that the meeting was over. "I have several errands to run. Also, the paints that I've ordered for Logan should be arriving tomorrow. I had them delivered to the museum since we did not have a delivery address yet for where we are staying. Could you let me know when they're here?"

"Of course," Dulcie said as she also pushed back her chair and stood. "Let me know if there's anything else," she said somewhat curtly as she walked Linda to the door.

"Yes, I will," Linda replied flatly, and left.

Dulcie closed the door behind her and went to the window. She opened it and inhaled deeply. "Who's in charge here, damn it?" she said out loud. A knock sounded at the door. "Come in!" she called impatiently.

Rachel, Dulcie's assistant, opened the door and stepped in. She took one look at Dulcie and closed the door behind her. "So that went well?" she said with a bemused face.

Dulcie leaned against the wide windowsill and dragged her hands over her face. "What have I done?!" Her voice moaned from beneath them.

Rachel giggled and Dulcie uncovered her face. "Only *you* are allowed to laugh because you've actually dealt with them, too!" She shook her head in dismay.

Rachel handed Dulcie some papers. "You won't like these either, then. Invoices for the paints that Logan Dumbarton needed. Along with more canvases and a special stool. The ones we have here aren't adjustable."

Dulcie looked at them and gasped. "Seriously? This is costing us a small fortune! And now we can't add any more students to the class, either. How am I going to tell the board?"

"You'll think of something," said Rachel. "You always do. Maybe we should get a cheaper champagne for the reception?"

Dulcie looked thoughtful. "Actually, that's not a bad idea. I'd budgeted for a bit of a splurge there since we had such a noted artist. Frankly, I don't think he's worth it now."

"Should I still get your standard bottle to bury at the bottom of the ice?" Rachel asked.

Dulcie laughed. Each time she dug her favorite champagne out from the ice at the end of a long night, she always remembered her old friend, Joshua Harriman, the man who had recruited her and taught her that trick. "Something to look forward to. A little reward for hard work. It makes all that schmoozing *nearly* worth the trouble," he had once said. His bottle of choice had always been some vintage of Dom Pérignon. Dulcie's was Veuve Clicquot Ponsardin, otherwise known as The Widow. She wished she had a glass now.

"Rachel, you know me too well," she replied.

Rachel giggled again. "Good. I'll look at the catering menu and see if we can cut any corners there too. Without being obvious, of course!"

"Of course," replied Dulcie. "Thank you, Rachel. I couldn't do any of this without you," she said, scrawling her signature on the invoices for approval and handing them back.

"I know!" Rachel said over her shoulder as she opened the door. She turned. "Open or shut?" she asked.

"Shut! Please!" Dulcie replied.

Rachel grinned one last time and closed the door.

*An artist cannot fail;
it is a success to be one.*
~ Charles Horton Cooley

CHAPTER THREE

Seven people sat quietly in the room, nervously adjusting their tubes of paints, selecting and putting down brushes, and glancing up at the clock. It was one minute after ten o'clock and their teacher, the great artist Logan Dumbarton, had yet to make his appearance. One student murmured something in a low voice and the two on either side laughed nervously.

Upstairs, Dulcie had just received word from Rachel that Logan had not yet arrived. Dulcie quickly hurried down to the studio. She came in apologizing for his tardiness and attempted to begin the class. Or at least kill time.

"Let's start with some quick introductions. I'm sure Mr. Dumbarton will want to hear more about all of you, so we'll save longer ones for when he arrives. How about if we go around the room with names? I'll start. I'm Dulcie Chambers." Everyone laughed. They all knew who she was.

The man on her left spoke up. "Scott Adams," he said in a low, gentle voice. He was wearing an old pair of khakis and a polo shirt that had seen many washings.

"I'm Tara Stevenson, and this is my sister Mary," said the young woman beside Scott. She gestured toward the woman on the other side of her.

"We're twins, but you'd never know it," Mary said. Everyone laughed again; both girls had exactly the same golden-blonde wavy hair, blue eyes, and large smiles.

"How do people tell you apart?" asked Scott.

"On the second try," quipped Tara. More chuckles from her classmates.

The man on Tara's left spoke up. "I'm Bryce Bartlett. I have no twin. That would've killed my mother!" Dulcie looked over at him. He was probably in his thirties and wore a Red Sox baseball cap. His t-shirt read, *'Can't drink all day...'* on the front, and *'... if you don't start in the morning!'* on the back. She was inclined to agree with his sentiment about his mother.

The last three people introduced themselves. Kimberly Whittimore appeared to be in her sixties, with smooth gray hair cut in a bob. *'Very sensible,'* thought Dulcie. Bethany Blakely was probably fortyish, wore perfectly creased jeans, and had her paint tubes lined up neatly, all in the same direction, in her wooden paint box. *'Too precise for a class focusing on abstract art,'* Dulcie thought. She wondered why Bethany had signed up, but perhaps she was trying to push herself. She already looked uncomfortable. The final student was Willow, "Just *Willow*." She gave no last name, although Dulcie had seen it on her registration form. She looked nothing like a *Willow*. She was androgynous with arms covered in tattoos, including several prominent skulls. Her nose was pierced with a small spike that appeared to be embellished with a diamond on the end.

As they finished, Logan Dumbarton edged into the room. His sister followed him. He carefully put down the small bag that he was carrying and gestured for her to put the other, much larger bags that she carried, in the corner. "Ah," he said. "I see everyone is here. Very good. I am Logan Dumbarton. Let's begin with a discussion of the color blue."

Dulcie was shocked. She had never seen such a transformation. The suave man she had met previously was nowhere to be found. Instead, this version of Logan Dumbarton had dark circles under his eyes, a slightly bent back as though it had spent too many hours leaning over a canvas, and a voice accompanied by frequent snuffles into his handkerchief.

Dulcie looked over at Linda to see if she would acknowledge anything amiss. Linda simply scribbled in her notebook as she usually did, ignoring everyone. Dulcie edged over to her, and gestured for them to step into the hallway. Linda took off her reading glasses and followed.

In the hallway Dulcie whispered, "Is Logan all right?"

Linda looked confused. "Of course he is. Why do you ask?"

As she had before, Dulcie abandoned all pretense. She was quickly learning that the straightforward approach with this strange group was probably the best. "I ask because he looks terrible!"

"Oh, that!" Linda waved her hand. "Sometimes he stays up very late working. He always looks wretched in the morning afterward. He's fine, though. I make sure he has everything he needs. He's just so fragile, you know."

Dulcie was silent. She did not know what to say. She looked back into the room. The students all seemed attentive to his lecture, so Dulcie guessed there really was no reason to interrupt. She did find it odd, and even rude, that he had not bothered with introductions so that he could learn the students' names. He had not apologized for being late either.

Feeling annoyed, Dulcie decided to address the latter issue. "Did you have trouble getting here this morning?" she asked.

Again, Linda's face registered confusion. "No, no trouble at all."

"It's just that the class was scheduled to begin at ten o'clock," Dulcie said.

Now Linda looked annoyed. "Please tell me that you did not expect an artist, especially one of Logan's stature, to arrive on time! It was all I could do to get him going this morning!" She glared at Dulcie and without waiting for another word went back into the studio.

⚃

Dulcie sat on her brother's yacht holding a glass of sparkling wine.

"Well, you've been told!" he said, futilely attempting to hide a smile. Dan Chambers had just returned from his final trip of the day, taking tourists around the bay for what he termed his "champagne cruise." He and Dulcie were partners in his business although he ran it entirely. She had invested the capital to buy the boat after receiving an unexpected inheritance. Dan lived on board and docked near the museum, which was convenient for Dulcie. She was a frequent visitor.

She laughed. "It's the strangest thing I've ever seen! One day he's a suave, arrogant, overbearing, annoying, ..."

"I get the picture," interjected Dan.

"The next, he's a sniveling, sickly, bent-over wreck! And his sister seems to think it's perfectly normal!"

"Maybe it is, for her."

"Dan, that can't be normal! For anyone!"

Dan just laughed. He poured a glass of wine for himself from the last bottle. "Might's well finish this off," he said.

"The truth is," she continued, ignoring him, "I don't know what to do with them. We made it through the first class, but the next one will be outdoors, and I'm not sure at all how that will go over."

Dan leaned back against a life vest and put his feet up on a battered cooler. His docksiders were perfectly worn, adding to his overall 'ship's captain' look. "Dulcie, did you ever consider that you might be overthinking this? Yes, he's a character. They all sound like characters. But as long as the students are happy, then the class is a success, right?"

Dulcie sighed. "Yes, I suppose you're right. Are you saying that I'm being overly attentive to detail?"

Dan grinned. "You? Never!"

She leaned over and swatted him on the arm.

"Hey, don't spill the good stuff!" he said nearly dumping his glass over.

"Dan, this is total crap, and you know it!"

"You're drinking it," he replied.

Now Dulcie laughed. Dan always knew what to say. Although Dulcie was undeniably the practical sibling,

Dan's inherent wisdom seemed to override her worrisome nature on many occasions. She sighed once again. "Even though Logan and his entourage have been a pain to deal with, it's good to have a distraction. And to be busy," she said.

Dan looked more serious now. "Dulcie, I was worried when you went away to Bermuda like that."

Dan never worried. Dulcie was surprised. "I told you where I was going, what I was doing…"

"Yeah, I know. But I haven't seen you like that before."

Dulcie had never felt like that, either. It confused her. Although she had no real reason, she had felt betrayed.

As if reading her mind, Dan said, "Want me to punch him?"

Dulcie nearly snorted sparkling wine from her nose. She swallowed hard and laughed loudly. "Dan, this isn't the Middle Ages!"

"It's what guys do. It settles the score."

"It is not what *civilized* guys do, and I will not have you going around punching people simply to defend my honor! Especially not members of the police force."

"Oh yeah, I forgot about that part."

Dulcie shook her head. "Besides, he did nothing."

"What? He led you on!" Dan replied adamantly. "I saw it! He was interested in you…"

"Yes, maybe he was, but he didn't *do* anything about it, and that's the whole point. Can we just drop it? I'd like Nicholas Black to be in the past now. Neither of us has any reason to see him again unless, heaven forbid, we bump into him somewhere."

"All right. I won't mention him. But if I do bump into him, he might get the verbal equivalent of a punch."

"Dan! Don't even think about it!"

Her brother laughed and finished his drink. "Want me to walk you home?"

"Thanks, but no. It's a nice evening, still bright, and I need to think. I do appreciate the advice though, and the wine," she said. She handed him her glass and stepped up onto the dock.

Dan smiled. "It's *champagne*," he said.

CB

Linda pulled the elastic band out of her hair and dragged a brush through it. She looked at herself in the mirror. A lifetime dedicated to managing her brother's career, and what had it brought her? Certainly not fame and fortune. That was his department. She simply paved the way, removed the obstacles, ensured that nothing would inhibit his flow of creativity and affect his work. It was a thankless job.

She paid herself well enough. Logan didn't care what she took for money as long as he had more than plenty for himself. Yet what did she have to spend it on? Where did she ever go? What did she ever do? She had given up on nice clothes. She looked in the mirror at her hair. Evidently she had given up on nice haircuts as well.

She put down the brush and pulled her hair severely back again into the elastic. She thought about Isabel's hair. Always silky and exotic looking, even when pulled back like Linda's was now. She doubted that Isabel had ever looked plain a day in her life.

Everything had changed the day that Isabel had come into their lives. Why had Linda encouraged her brother to go to that damned party? He hadn't wanted to go in the first place, but she knew there would be potential buyers stopping by, and interest in Logan's work had been slowing a bit lately. Unfortunately, he had never even spoken to them. He had simply stared at Isabel.

Linda shook her head vigorously, stuffing the thoughts in the back of her mind again. She needed to focus. The previous evening had been a long one. Logan had wanted gin and tonics, one after another. They were his drink of choice. Then he and Isabel retreated to the bedroom. Linda stayed up for another hour trying to plan how their time in Maine would unfold. She was about to go to bed when Logan staggered out of the room in his robe and *suggested* another drink, along with a ham sandwich. That's how he always put it, as a *suggestion*. Linda knew orders when she heard them. After several more drinks, he eventually went to bed again. Linda wondered how Isabel could possibly be putting up with him.

Logan's *suggestions* had become more frequent since marrying Isabel. His wife did little for him, barely lifting a finger. She seemed to whine more than anything else. Yet, like Logan, Linda found it difficult to take her eyes off Isabel whenever she was in the room. She had magnetism, a way of dominating her surroundings that was almost frightening. Linda wasn't even sure if Isabel was aware of it herself, although she suspected that she was. Girls learn quickly how to use their attributes to their advantage, especially when exotic beauty is one of them.

The marriage was odd to anyone who knew him. Logan had never shown an inclination to get married, and after he had turned forty, Linda had simply assumed that he would be a bachelor all his life. Yet, she understood how he could become enraptured with Isabel — anyone at the general age of a midlife crisis could be lured by a woman like that — but what was in it for Isabel herself? There was a bit of fame, certainly, and the fortune. Yet it seemed like a large price to pay for those things.

Linda heard a car crunch into the gravel driveway. She quickly went to the kitchen and began preparing a spinach salad with mandarin oranges and a light balsamic vinaigrette. It was his *suggestion* for dinner.

The greater the artist,
the greater the doubt.
Perfect confidence is granted
to the less talented
as a consolation prize.
~ Robert Hughes

CHAPTER FOUR

The Logan Dumbarton master class had their first experience of *plein air* painting with the famed artist on the following Monday. Dulcie had breathed a huge sigh of relief when the first studio class had ended well. The students had even been able to use their paints although blue seemed to be the only color that was allowed on the canvas.

Dulcie sat in a metal lawn chair in the front yard of Logan Dumbarton's rented house. It had been Linda's idea to hold *plein air* sessions there. Dulcie had quickly agreed. The students had a spectacular view of the ocean, facilities available as needed in the house and, most important of all as far as Dulcie was concerned, Logan had no excuse to be late for his own class.

The students were scattered across the lawn, each with a slightly different view of the ocean. The lawn dropped off to rocks below that led to a small, pebbled beach. Dulcie would have liked to try her hand at painting as well — she had worked with oils in college — but decided it was best to oversee and make sure the class stayed on track. She did not yet trust Logan Dumbarton to carry everything through, and Linda seemed to think that his behavior was perfectly acceptable.

As Dulcie looked around she saw Isabel emerge from the house. The day was very warm; most of the artists were wearing hats and plenty of sunscreen. Isabel wore nothing but a very tiny leopard-print bikini. She was carrying a drink of some kind with fruit on the top and a towel draped over her arm. "Logan, darling!" she called out.

Everyone turned and looked at her. Paintbrushes remained poised in midair. She appeared not to notice that she was now the center of attention. Logan came running over. Earlier that morning, when he had first appeared, he was the bent, shuffling, sickly looking middle-aged man that Dulcie had seen during the first class session. Apparently, in spite of appearances, he was still capable of moving quickly.

Isabel gestured lazily. Logan moved a chaise around into the sun and spread the towel over it. Most of the artists turned back to their work as Isabel settled in, however both Bryce and Scott continued to gawk. Bryce finally reached up and adjusted his ever-present baseball cap before picking up a brush and looking at the ocean again. Scott heaved a deep sigh, then shifted in his seat so that Isabel was out of his range of vision.

Dulcie stood, deciding to walk among the artists and see how they were progressing. As she did, Linda appeared in the window. She did not seem to notice Dulcie. Instead, she stared intently at Isabel. *I wonder how strongly Linda dislikes her?* Dulcie thought. *Is it simply annoyance, or has she reached the point of hatred yet?*

Dulcie continued to wander around the lawn. She stopped and spoke with each of the students. Mary and Tara were sitting near enough to each other so that they could chat from time to time. "How are you two doing?" asked Dulcie.

"Great!" they said in unison, then giggled.

"We were just wondering if we would end up with exactly the same painting," said Mary.

"Now that would be scary!" Dulcie said. "Do you often work together?"

Tara answered, "Actually, no. We both just got back from internships. I was in Los Angeles and Mary was in New York, so we haven't seen much of each other for a while. That's why we decided to take this class together."

"I'm glad we could fit both of you in," said Dulcie. "Where are you going to school?"

"We're both at PCA." Mary said.

Dulcie knew PCA, the Portland College of Art, very well. She looked back and forth between the girls, wondering if they always took turns speaking. She asked one more question to test her theory, predicting that Tara would be next. "How much longer do you have before graduation?" she asked, looking pointedly at Mary.

Tara answered, "One more year."

Dulcie smiled. She would have liked to see if the volley would continue but thought it better to move on. "Glad things are going well," she said.

"Thanks!" they said in unison.

Dulcie reached Kimberly who had just taken off her hat. Her gray hair was now a gleaming silver in the sunlight. Adjusting her sunglasses, she looked up at Dulcie. "The only trouble I have with *plein air*, is that when I wear these glasses, I don't see colors right," she said. "But, my eyes are so sensitive to bright light that I need them, or I'll have tears streaming down my face, and that would never do!" she laughed.

"Logan would tell you to '*abstract with that*,' I think," said Dulcie. They had heard the phrase several times already.

Kimberly laughed again. It was a soft, bubbly sound that made Dulcie smile. "Yes, he certainly would. Although I think that right now he wouldn't notice a thing that any of us said or did." She was looking beyond Dulcie in the direction of Isabel's chaise. Dulcie turned. Logan was adjusting his wife's towel.

"Yes. Between you and me, this class has been quite different from what I anticipated." She looked back at Kimberly. Something about her seemed very trustworthy. "Could I ask a favor of you?" Dulcie said.

"Of course," Kimberly said, putting down her brush and wiping her hands with a rag. "You sound very serious! What is it?"

"I suppose I am very serious. I shouldn't put this on your shoulders since you're here to learn and enjoy the class, but I'm wondering if you could be my confidant?" Dulcie asked. "I won't be able to observe every class. In fact, I hadn't planned on observing any of them beyond a simple check-in from time to time. If I'm not around, could you please let me know if things aren't going well? I want all of the students to feel as though this was worth their time. And money, for that matter."

Kimberly nodded. "I would be happy to, although I've never been the class snitch! And I've certainly never snitched on the teacher!"

"I can't imagine you've ever been a snitch in any way at all," said Dulcie. Kimberly appeared so genuine and approachable. Dulcie imagined that she would have been the one to sort out any problem rather than report it.

"It's always fun to play a different part, though, isn't it?" Kimberly said. She took off her glasses and looked back at her painting. "Never fear! I'll keep an eye out for you!" She winked confidentially at Dulcie.

Dulcie thanked her and moved on. She was approaching Bryce from behind when he suddenly stood and strode quickly across the grass. Logan had begun circulating between the artists again, shuffling along, speaking in a low voice. Isabel was sipping her drink alone in silence. Bryce slowed his pace when he reached her and said something. Dulcie couldn't hear them, but Isabel giggled. As she did, Logan looked up sharply. He stared intently at the two. Bryce spoke again, then walked around the house and pulled a folding chair from the back of his truck.

Logan scurried back to Isabel. Dulcie saw them exchanging somber words. *'So jealousy rears it's ugly head!'* she thought. As she watched the pair, she saw the curtains move in the window behind them. Linda was standing in exactly the same spot as before, still staring at Isabel.

CB

The second *plein air* session of the Logan Dumbarton Master Class was held the next day. It had rained the night before so students were attempting to keep as much of their art paraphernalia off the wet grass as possible. Bethany had the foresight to bring a large blanket. She had spread it out first, then returned to her car for all of her gear. The items that she brought along, all strapped to a rolling luggage cart, were considerable. It took at least ten minutes for her to set up her chair, easel, a large umbrella with a clamp apparatus, and a side table for her paints that were, of course, precisely aligned. Bethany also had a small cooler. Dulcie was dying to know what was in it. She could picture a perfectly constructed sandwich.

Willow analyzed the arrangement. She wished she'd thought to bring a beach towel. She glanced over at Bryce who had walked up next to her. He cocked his head to one side, considering Bethany's setup as well. "Man, she is *way* too tight," he said under his breath.

Willow snorted. "Yeah. But it isn't entirely a bad idea. I mean, the blanket was pretty smart." She looked around at the wet grass.

Bryce shook his head. "Just ignore it. It'll be dry soon enough. Here, I'll help you with this stuff." He put all of his own things on the damp ground and took her easel from her. "Where do you want this?"

Willow was surprised. It was rare that anyone was helpful with her. She knew that she was looking especially spikey today, too. Bryce didn't even seem to notice. "Um, over here. I was looking in that direction last time."

Bryce obliged, setting up the easel and turning it so that she had the proper view. "All set?" he asked.

Willow smiled. It was a rare occurrence, and it changed her entire face. She looked younger, childlike, as though her rough exterior was just a game of dress-up. "Yup, all set. Thanks, Bryce!"

He nodded, grabbed his things and sauntered off to the location he'd been positioned at during the previous class. Willow wished that he had stayed near her.

Dulcie arrived as the students were setting up. Scott had moved closer to the twins, and she could hear them chatting. Dulcie had learned that he was a part-time instructor at PCA, so he probably knew them previously. Once you met Mary and Tara, they were hard to forget.

Dulcie located Kimberly and walked gingerly through the wet grass toward her. As she passed Bethany, nodding a greeting, Dulcie caught Kimberly's eye. Dulcie mouthed "Wow!" and Kimberly turned to hide her smile.

When Dulcie reached her, Kimberly was trying not to laugh. "It appears that Bethany is a planner!" she said.

"She certainly leaves nothing to chance," Dulcie replied.

"At least I thought to bring a towel, so that's something," said Kimberly. "It seems that everyone is settling in. We haven't seen the Great One yet, but I imagine he'll be shuffling out in a few moments. I've seen some movement inside, so at least they're up and about."

Dulcie turned toward the house just in time to see the door open. Logan Dumbarton stepped out and quickly closed it behind him, but not before Dulcie could see Linda and Isabel inside. They appeared to be arguing.

'Odd,' thought Dulcie. '*I didn't think they even spoke to one another.*'

She moved closer to the house. Logan looked unflustered. He gave her a condescending smile, bordering on a sneer, as he brushed by. '*I see we're having a suave day, not a sickly day,*' thought Dulcie. Then she realized that she needed to be careful. She had never been able to conceal her emotions. *Which is why I could never beat Dan at cards,'* she remembered.

Dulcie walked around the front steps of the house and leaned against the railing so that she couldn't be seen well from the windows. To anyone looking, she appeared to be observing Scott and the twins painting nearby. In fact, she was listening intently.

"...don't care how long you and he have been together! I'm his wife! You'll do as I say..."

Dulcie missed the last bit. She couldn't hear Linda's reply, either. A few moments later she heard the back door slam, and saw Isabel quickly drive off. *'Trouble in paradise,'* thought Dulcie. *'Three's a crowd.'*

Logan had been speaking to Willow. Dulcie saw a dark look spread across the girl's face. Her eyes had narrowed until they were just tiny slits among the piercings on her eyebrows. She looked as though she would claw and eat him. Dulcie watched her turn and walk slowly to the edge of the lawn where she stayed for several moments, facing the ocean.

Logan strode up to Bethany. He spoke to her in a low voice for several moments. He pointed to the towel and the umbrella and laughed. It was a nasty sound.

Bethany slowly put down her brush. Logan snatched it up, smashed it into a large amount of yellow paint, then proceeded to blob it onto the canvas in several places. Bethany gasped. He ignored her and swirled it around and around. Where it mixed with the blue it blended to an unattractive bright green. He tossed the brush back on her palette where the long handle of it stuck right in the middle of the paint.

Bethany looked as though she would burst into tears. As Dulcie hurried over she heard Logan's condescending chuckle. He sauntered away in the direction of Bryce. Dulcie ran up to Bethany and put a consoling arm around her shoulders. Tears were in Bethany's eyes, and she quickly put on her sunglasses. "He didn't even ask!" she sniffed. "I mean, I know he's the great artist, but it's polite to ask if you can touch someone else's painting! I thought I was doing pretty well!" She choked back a little hiccupping sob.

"What did he say?" Dulcie asked.

"He said that I would never be any good. He said that I tried too hard, that I'm too rigid!" Bethany's dismay began to morph into anger. "He said it in such an awful, arrogant voice. Like he's so much better just because he's a professional artist and I'm just a... just a..." She couldn't finish.

"Just a very talented and very nice person who is capable of enjoying herself without putting down others," Dulcie finished for her.

Bethany sniffed loudly. She took off her sunglasses and wiped her eyes. "Thank you. I needed to hear that."

Dulcie looked at the painting. "You know, you could sell this for a pretty good amount of money. It's a joint piece now, a Bethany-Logan." She was trying desperately to interject some humor.

Bethany tried to laugh. "As long as I get top billing, I suppose that would be okay."

Dulcie noticed her bag of supplies. She had another blank canvas in it. "Want to start over?" she asked, reaching for it.

"*Yes!*" said Bethany. She grabbed the ruined canvas and, to Dulcie's surprise, blithely tossed it, face-down, so that it skidded across the wet grass. "There! That felt good!" She looked over at Dulcie and giggled.

Dulcie gave Bethany a pat on the back and stepped away. She looked around for Logan again to see who he would be accosting next. He was with Bryce. They appeared to be discussing something very intently. Willow had edged over, obviously to listen. She silently moved back to her painting when she saw Dulcie approaching.

"Everything going well?" Dulcie asked, trying to sound breezy.

"Why wouldn't it be?" said Willow defensively.

Dulcie raised her eyebrows, then wished she hadn't. It would only draw Willow's ire. "At least we have another nice day," she said, seeking a less provoking topic. Weather was always benign.

"You can call it that if you want," Willow said, without looking at her.

Dulcie decided not to take the bait. "Do you like what you've been working on so far?" she asked.

Willow dropped both arms to her sides and glared at Dulcie. "Yeah. I do. Or I did. Until *he* came along with his 'constructive criticism.' I'm nothing but a copycat, it seems. No hint of the genius in me. But that's OK, he says, because we all can't be great like him. And imitation is the most sincere form of compliment."

"Is that what he said?" Dulcie asked.

"Something like that. The last sentence was verbatim. The rest was along those lines. And he said it in such a backhanded, put-down way. You know what I mean? You don't know he's just slammed you until you think about it, after he's gone. You know, this master class would be great... without the master."

"Willow, it's all about attitude, and you have plenty of that." Dulcie saw Willow narrow her eyes. "I mean that in a good way. Attitude is what sells your work. I've seen a lot of talented artists who made it nowhere because they had no personality. Even if it's an abrasive personality, it makes you stand out from all the rest. If you're a contemporary artist, half of what makes your work sell is who you are. The other half is the talent."

"What if you're a dead artist?" said Willow scornfully, eyeing Logan across the lawn.

Dulcie laughed. "Then it's just luck."

Willow snorted, and began mixing a new color on her palette. It resembled a blood red.

Logan had left Bryce and had circulated around to Scott and the twins. Kimberly had joined them, holding her canvas. *'Smart lady,'* thought Dulcie. *'She saw what was happening. Safety in numbers.'* She heard the group laugh and knew that Logan could not get away with his condescending remarks now that so many of them were gathered together. He worked best one-on-one.

Dulcie quietly approached Bryce. "So you've received an in-depth analysis of your work?" she asked.

Her question lacked innocence and she knew it. Bryce chuckled. "I give as good as I get. He won't be talking with me again anytime soon, most likely. At least, he won't be giving me any 'helpful tips' regarding my career."

"Then this class won't be very worthwhile for you, I'm afraid."

Bryce continued painting. "On the contrary," he said without looking up. "It is very helpful. I get to watch a master in action. And he is truly a master. If only he could paint."

೮೮

Isabel Dumbarton drove without thinking. Or rather, she drove without thinking about where she was. She was most certainly thinking.

Linda had become a problem. Isabel had never encountered difficulty getting what she wanted in her entire life. It all seemed to come her way. Born in India, she had been adopted by a wealthy British couple. They had died tragically in a car crash when she was only seventeen. She had inherited everything. Yet, in the span of ten years, without the counsel of parents, or any family for that matter, Isabel had managed to spend most of the money.

One's needs at seventeen are very different from one's needs at twenty-seven. When she realized that the money was dwindling, Isabel had been able to develop a small career as a model. She looked younger than her actual age and frequently lied about it. Her dark, exotic appearance was the current trend, and she worked that to her advantage. She was too petite for fashion or runway work, but she had been photographed for several cosmetic and jewelry advertising campaigns, and was even the face beneath a line of hats. It was enough to keep her solvent for the time being, but she knew that the work would not last forever.

Never would she have considered herself to be a gold-digger. After all, she had not sought out Logan Dumbarton. She did not consider marrying him to be entirely an act of greed and self-promotion. She liked to view it as an opportunity. Although she could not say that she was attracted to him, she did admire him in an odd way. His life seemed so exciting. In their first conversation he told her that she instantly had inspired him to begin working in a new direction. He told her that she was magical, truly his muse. He begged her to be with him. Then he begged her to marry him. Her ego could not say no. Neither could her bank account.

She drove with the windows down and the sea air whipping through the car. The excitement with Logan had begun to wane. Now she felt trapped. And Linda! At first it was nice to have someone else worrying about all of life's little details. Now she was a hovering presence, constantly watching. With all of them crammed together in one little house, Isabel found that hatred was creeping in to her world.

Something else was there as well. Isabel had been entirely on her own for so long that she had learned to sense even the smallest changes in people. Logan was different since they had come to Maine. He was drinking more, certainly. Lately, he had been Arrogant Logan more often than Sickly Logan. What had brought this about? Was it Isabel herself? Did she feed his arrogance? Linda certainly fed his sickly nature, always responding to his silly, pathetic needs.

Isabel did not want to admit it to herself, but that *something else* that she felt was fear. She tried to brush it aside and to tell herself that it was just a silly reaction to all of the change in her life. There was nothing to fear, really. She told herself that she was simply in a situation that she had never before encountered. It was natural to feel uncomfortable. Perhaps she was confusing that feeling with fear. Yes, that was it.

She didn't enjoy whining. Isabel knew that she had been doing far too much of it lately. Yet, it seemed to be the only thing that would elicit any kind of response from Logan. Logan was a whiner when he was in his sickly moods. Whining seemed to be his predominant mode of communication. Whenever she attempted to talk with him in a regular manner, to comment on his work or ask a question, he would make a condescending remark. "You just don't understand, my pet. You are so adorably naïve." Those were standard phrases. Then he would give her a peck on the cheek or, worse, pat her head. She felt like a lap dog.

The words that the nagging voice in her head uttered over and over were simple: *get me out!* She could not quite bring herself to act on them, however.

❧

By Wednesday the mood among the students in Logan Dumbarton's Master Class in Abstract Painting had changed considerably. Three had suffered through his humiliating commentary of their work. The remaining four knew it was only a matter of time before their turn would come.

Tara and Mary were uncharacteristically silent, as they sat dabbing at their canvases. In spite of his experience as a teacher himself, Scott paced in front of his easel. He occasionally stopped, stared out at the ocean, picked up his brush, then put it down again. All three knew that the storm cloud was threatening, yet they still analyzed their work, wondering exactly what Logan the Great would find wrong with it.

Only Kimberly appeared unflustered. She worked calmly, holding her brush with a steady hand, mixing colors, and applying paint as she best saw fit. She considered herself lucky. Her primary motivation for being there no longer was to perfect her technique. No, her motivation was to observe, analyze, and perhaps even predict what would happen next. Painting was secondary.

She stopped only briefly to look back at the house when she heard the front door open. One glance was enough to tell her that most likely she, and everyone else, would be safe for today. A snuffling and sickly Logan had emerged.

He shuffled over to Kimberly first. Honking his nose loudly into a crumpled handkerchief he muttered, "Fine. Your blues are good. Representational. Not literal. Watch the lines here," he dabbed his finger into the paint on the canvas, then wiped it on his shirt.

Kimberly slowly extended her brush and swept it over his fingerprint. He appeared not to notice. He nodded his head over and over. Kimberly thought that he had begun some sort of convulsion and would, at any moment, fall to the ground in a writhing fit.

He did not. Instead, he turned abruptly, coughed loudly, and scuffled over to Scott. Kimberly couldn't hear what was said, but she assumed he received the same treatment form the great master. She glanced over several times, her eyes straining to one side so that she wouldn't have to move her head. Scott did not appear to be distressed.

A dual personality. That seemed to be the key to Logan Dumbarton. But was it truly a psychological aberration, or was he simply worn down at times by work, drink, sleep deprivation, or whatever else was happening in his life? And which was his true personality? Kimberly couldn't be sure.

She put down her brush and stretched. It was a ruse to look around the lawn at her fellow students. As she did, Linda hurried out of the house. She held a glass of something that resembled tomato juice with a large plastic straw in it. When she reached Logan, he took it without acknowledging her presence. She quietly walked backwards away from him, never taking her eyes off him.

Logan ignored the straw and took several large gulps. He closed his eyes for a moment and swayed from side to side. He raised the glass again, attempting to find the straw with his mouth without opening his eyes. His distorted lips located it at last, and he sipped slowly, draining half the glass before opening his eyes again. Color had come into his face and he seemed to have increased in height.

At that moment Linda passed by Kimberly. "Linda, what's in that drink?" she blurted out without thinking.

Linda did not stop. She continued to walk backwards. When she was almost beyond earshot, Kimberly heard her whisper, "tomato juice, raw egg, Tabasco, and a large shot of vodka."

'So that's it,' thought Kimberly. She had seen it before. Alcohol brought out the devil in some people, and made everyone else's world a living hell. Linda scurried back into the house. Logan finished his drink, then hurled the glass out toward the ocean. It shattered on the pebble beach. The twins were closest and both gasped. Logan turned slowly and eyed both of them.

"Which of you is older?" he asked quietly.

The twins looked at each other, then back at him. It was an odd question. "Technically, I am," said Tara. "But only by about ten minutes."

"It shows. Your work is slightly more mature. But that's not saying much." He turned his back to them and gazed at the horizon.

Mary and Tara moved their heads back in forth, nearly in unison, comparing each other's work. Neither knew what to say. Feeling that it must be her duty since she was just defined as the eldest, Tara said, "What exactly determines whether a work is mature or immature? If it's abstract, isn't that up to the observer to decide?"

Logan chuckled his low, condescending laugh. "You see," he said, "That's exactly the problem. The work has nothing to do with who observes it. It's what the artist chooses to project." He quickly turned, grabbed Mary's canvas, and flung it like a Frisbee across the beach. It floated in the shallow surf, then disappeared with the next large wave. Both girls watched it bob up again, floating further out.

"Now there's a distinct improvement!" Logan continued. "If you're producing total crap, you have to just let it go. Cast it aside! Begin again!"

Mary opened her mouth, but no words emerged. *'Total crap?'* she thought. *'But, why?'*

As if reading Mary's mind, Tara said, "And what exactly led you to the conclusion that it was *total crap?*"

Slowly, Logan turned. He did not look at her. Instead, he fixated on a point in the sky somewhere over her head. "One just knows," he said acidly. "Isn't it obvious?" His eyes lowered and met hers. "But then, I suppose for *you*," he gestured to the students around him, "well, let's just say you'll never know. Pity really, but none of you will ever make it." He turned on his heel and walked back toward the house.

Scott came running up to the twins. "Mary, your painting isn't that far out. I can get it for you! I thought it was really good, and it won't really be damaged that much…"

"No, that's OK. I'll just start over," Mary said in a small, wavering voice.

"Look, Mary, I may not be as famous as Logan Dumbarton, but I am a professional artist. What you had started was certainly quite good. Don't listen to him," Scott nearly pleaded with Mary.

Mary fought back tears. She had often wondered if she should really be pursuing a career in art. Tara was the talented one. Her works just emerged from the canvas. She never appeared to put in effort at all. Mary knew that her own work was the result of great labor. She loved it, but it was not easy.

Scott had seen that. He had taught for long enough to recognize those who worked, those who struggled, and those who simply created as a natural part of their lives. Tara simply created. Mary was somewhere between working and struggling.

Tears began streaming down Mary's face as she watched her painting bob up and down in the ocean. Without thinking Scott pulled her toward him, turning her away from that awful scene. He wrapped his arms around her and she sobbed into his chest. *'I'll kill him,'* he thought. *'No one should get away with that. No one should suffocate her sheer will to create.'*

Kimberly watched the entire scene. She carefully noted the details. One by one, the students picked up their brushes again and continued with their work. Kimberly edged herself from her chair and went to her car. Getting in, she clicked the door closed as quietly as possible. She slumped down in the seat so that she could just peak over the dashboard to watch the house. Then she dialed Dulcie's number.

Twenty minutes later, Dulcie pulled into the driveway of the Dumbarton's rented house. She tried to appear calm. She wanted everyone to think that she had just stopped by. As she passed the house, she knocked on the door. Linda opened it.

"Yes?" she said, without any attempt at a greeting.

"I'm just stopping in to see the students' progress. Is Logan on the lawn with them?"

Linda hesitated. "Uh, no. He came back in to lie down. He has a splitting headache."

Dulcie shook her head. "So he's not teaching his own class today? The students are working on their own? Linda, I hired him to teach, not to sleep. Can't he take an aspirin like everyone else?"

Linda's eyes narrowed. She stepped outside and closed the door behind her. "How *dare* you! Do you have any idea who you're talking about? Do you have any idea how *lucky* you are to have him here in the first place? Who are you to tell *him* what to do?"

"May I remind you, that you contacted me to set up this class. It was your idea. The museum is paying you well and covering your somewhat exorbitant expenses. All I ask is that Logan teach this class as we agreed, and to show some respect to the students who, I might add, have also paid a great deal of money to be here!" She had blurted out more than she intended.

Show some respect. That was an interesting phrase to throw in, Linda thought. She had witnessed every one of Logan's distasteful interactions with the students. Today had been the worst. *'Someone must have ratted him out,'* she thought. She glanced at all of the students, until her eyes stopped at Kimberly.

"You are lucky to have him here at all. That's all I can say. If you want him out here right now, you'll have to drag him out yourself." Linda walked back into the house and decisively shut the door behind her.

Dulcie took a deep breath. Then another. She stepped off the porch and strode across the grass.

"Can I have everyone come over here for a moment?" she called out to all of the students. One by one, each put down brushes and palettes, and joined her. "I understand that the circumstances of this class have been, well, *trying* may be one way of putting it."

Willow snorted from the back of the group.

"If any of you would like to drop out of the class, you'll receive a full refund. I don't want anyone to continue with an uncomfortable situation. Just let me know your decisions as soon as you can."

The students looked at each other. Willow spoke up. "He's a total jerk, that's for sure. But I could use this on my scholarship applications if I'm going to get any decent funding."

"That's a really great point," Scott said. "It'll look good on my resume, even if he is a total ass."

Bryce had been remarkably silent. He waited until it appeared that no one else would speak up. Then he said, "What goes around, comes around. He'll get his. And I for one would like to be there when it happens. I'd even like to help the karma along a bit," he added ominously.

The entire situation was spinning out of control. Dulcie could feel it. The class was scheduled to continue through the following week, but she didn't see how that could happen. She imagined the students dropping out, one by one. She tried not to imagine the money that would have to be refunded, the Dumbarton expense that would have to be paid. *'At least I can withhold his stipend if he fails to fulfill our contract,'* she thought, but then realized that she would need to check with the museum's lawyer. Since he was also a member of the board, he would surely tell the others. Then the entire fiasco would be revealed before she would have time to prepare her own presentation of it, and the board would think that she was incompetent. It seemed hopeless.

"Don't give up." Kimberly stood beside her. "A miracle could happen. Maybe he'll come out that door, apologize, and be a ray of sunshine for the next week."

Dulcie laughed loudly in spite of herself. "You have no idea how much I needed that. I don't believe a word of it, but I needed to hear it."

"Well, situations often have a way of sorting themselves out. You did the right thing. Everyone has an out if they want it, but I doubt they'll take it. Call it morbid curiosity, but we all want to see how this turns out. It's like watching a train wreck."

"You've got the last part right, for sure!" Dulcie replied. "And I hope you're right about the rest. Thanks, Kimberly. You've been an enormous help."

"That's the fun of it," she said and went back to her painting.

❧

Bethany's ordered life had been shattered. It hadn't taken much. The criticism of Logan Dumbarton, watching him blob paint all over her work, had opened the floodgates. Since her divorce she had carefully constructed her world, aligning all of the pieces, keeping everything precise. That had changed in an instant.

She had tried to hold herself together. She still went to the painting class, but inwardly she seethed. Who was he to criticize her? He didn't even know her! Ironically, he had said almost the same things that her ex-husband had said. She tried too hard. She was too rigid, too tightly wound.

Looking back, Bethany should have seen the signs that her marriage was ending. Yet the first thing that she could recall was him coming home smelling odd. Finally, she had identified the odor. Paint. Since he was an accountant, she didn't think he would be coming into contact with it in his work. When she confronted him, initially he had lied. He said the office next to his was being renovated. Bethany wasn't buying that story. She pressed him further until she learned the ugly truth.

He had found someone else. She was Bethany's complete opposite. This woman was an artist, a painter. He found her attitude and lifestyle *'freeing'* he had said. *'Fine,'* Bethany thought. *'You can be free all you want.'* She met with her lawyer the next day.

She had been on her own for several months now. Bethany had never painted before, but lied about it so that she could get into the master class with Logan Dumbarton. She wanted to prove that she was just as good, that she could paint too. Yet when Logan's criticism had been so harsh, when he had ridiculed her and her work, it was too much. He had crossed the line.

Bethany wandered through the rooms of her perfect house. Everything was crisp, trim, clean, neat... all of those endless adjectives that she had found so comforting. Evidently *he* had found them restricting. When he left, he had simply packed one suitcase of his things. He wanted nothing to do with anything that had been their life together.

She picked up a sofa pillow and adjusted it on the couch. She stepped back, tipping her head slightly to make sure that it was correctly aligned.

The burning rage that came over her was sudden and impossible to predict. She grabbed the pillow and hurled it across the room. She did the same with another. She went to the kitchen and got a knife, then began stabbing and tearing apart all of the pillows, then the cushions on the sofa, then the chairs. She couldn't stop. She cut herself. Her hand bled on the chintz fabric. She felt herself crying and angrily wiped away tears.

When she had run out of pillows and cushions, she dropped the knife. Hearing it clatter to the floor, she began to sob. Her cheeks felt wet and her nose was running. She went into the bathroom to find the tissues, looked in the mirror and screamed. Her face was smeared with blood. Her hands were bloody. Then she remembered cutting herself.

Her body still shuddering with sobs, she turned on the cold water and let it run over her hands, numbing the pain. She splashed it on her face. It seemed to calm her and wake her up at the same time. She splashed and splashed for a long time, getting water on the floor, the mirror, the walls.

She finally stopped. She took the pristine, white towel from its rack and held it tightly against her cut hand. After a few moments, she took it away. The cut didn't seem to be very deep. It would heal. She looked at the crimson stain on the towel. It was an oddly shaped kind of swirl, fading at the edges.

Bethany stared, then began to laugh. There it was! Her art! She heard herself shrieking hysterically as she looked at the towel. She dabbed it again on her hand, then looked at the new stain. She was an artist! How funny was *that*!

There are painters who
transform the sun into a yellow spot,
but there are others who,
thanks to their art and intelligence,
transform a yellow spot into the sun.
~ Pablo Picasso

CHAPTER FIVE

The wind had howled all night. Dulcie wasn't quite sure, but she thought she might have had three hours of sleep. Cumulative, not continuous. Between the Logan Dumbarton situation, worries about budgets, and the wind, the night had been anything but restful.

On the way to her office she stopped at Dan's boat. "Anyone home?" she called out from the dock.

Dan poked his head out from the cabin. "Yeeup. Just made coffee. Want some?"

Dulcie looked at her watch. "Dammit! This thing stopped again. What time is it?"

Dan disappeared then reappeared within several seconds. "Seven-forty. You've got plenty of time."

Dulcie crossed her eyes at him. "I have about fifteen minutes. I'm supposed to be in the office by eight."

"Says who? The boss can't be late?"

Dulcie smiled. It was the first time she had done that in at least two days, she thought. Leave it to Dan.

"You're right. I can always call Rachel and tell her I'm in a meeting."

"Assuming she's on time," Dan replied.

"Rachel is always on time. One of the many things I love about her."

"And I love her bonny blue eyes, her radiant hair, her…"

"That's quite enough, Dan." Dulcie took the coffee he handed her. They both sat down in the cabin, escaping the wind outside. "No trips today?" She asked.

He shook his head swallowing a large mouthful of his own coffee vigorously. "Nope. Way too windy. It'll kick up a sea farther out, too and I'd have seasick folks for sure. Not worth it."

"I couldn't agree more, although I'm not sure how you do it, even on a good day." Dulcie was the introvert of the family. Dan was the complete opposite.

"Oh, they're fine. I like all their stories, for the most part. Always something different. Everyone seems to like mine, too."

"That's because you embellish," said Dulcie while blowing on her coffee.

Dan grinned. "Creative license. Makes for good entertainment. And speaking of entertainment, how's the situation with that artist?"

Dulcie leaned her head back and groaned.

"Oohh! It's better than ever, I see!"

"Dan, I really think it's out of control. He seems to have a split personality. One day he's sickly, the next he's an overbearing snob. Lately it's the latter, and he's managed to belittle nearly everyone in the class.

Yesterday he even threw one woman's painting into the ocean."

Dan's eyes were wide. "No! That's awful! How'd she take it?"

"Not well, that's for sure. Logan stormed back into the house. I wasn't there to see it. One of the other students called me right after, so I hurried over from the museum. When I knocked on the door of their house, Linda said that Logan had a headache and couldn't be disturbed. You can imagine how I reacted to that."

"Unfortunately, yes, I can."

"After that, I spoke to the students and said that they could drop the class with a full refund. No one seems to want to take that route yet. Dan, if they do, I have an enormous hole in the budget. The Dumbarton expenses have been huge, and even if I don't pay him the stipend, I'm in big trouble."

"Whoa, slow down! Dulcie, you're not there yet. Yes, good to have a Plan B always, but don't assume the worst. This all could blow over."

"I suppose so. I just have a really bad feeling about it."

"Don't buy trouble. You're such an eternal pessimist." Dulcie had heard that so many times from him. She tried to hide her smile with the coffee cup. Dan noticed. "Here's what you do," he continued, "Take one day at a time. Get yourself a nice big Chinese take-out dinner tonight, chicken fried rice and all, and don't think about anything. Read a good book. Otherwise you'll just fret."

"Yes. I know you're right."

"Of course I'm right. Now get the hell off my boat and go to work. I've got things to do!"

Dulcie laughed. "It's my boat, too!"

"You don't live here. Gimme that mug. Off with you!" He waved her away and opened the door. The wind howled through the cabin, as Dulcie stepped out. She climbed back up on the dock, waved to her brother, and hurried toward the museum.

Two hours later Dulcie was driving down the winding roads toward the ocean in Cape Elizabeth. She had not heard from Kimberly, so she assumed all was well. As she parked her car, she looked out across the lawn. The wind was still gusting, and many of the students had devised clever ways to hold their canvases in place. The twins had given up and were kneeling on the ground over theirs. They had held them down with rocks.

Dulcie subtly waved at Kimberly who smiled and nodded back. Dulcie quietly greeted the students as she wandered among them, making her way over toward Kimberly's direction. "Any sign of The Master?" Dulcie asked.

"Nope. Not yet. I've only just seen the curtains open. Maybe it was a late night for them."

"Unfortunately that always seems to be the case," Dulcie replied.

"You look tired," said Kimberly. "Late one for you? But not in a good way?" she asked.

"You could say that," said Dulcie. "The wind kept me awake. That, and worrying over this situation. My brother told me that I should have a big dinner along with a good book tonight and stop thinking about it."

"He's right, you know," Kimberly said. She had a comforting, motherly manner. She seemed to emit strength, and that's what Dulcie needed.

They both turned when they heard the door of the house open. To their surprise, Isabel stepped out. She wore blue jeans and a faded silky sweater. Logan was nowhere to be seen. Isabel carried a steaming cup of tea with her. Dulcie could see the paper tab on the end of the teabag string fluttering in the wind. Isabel sipped carefully.

She walked over to the twins and sat on the ground between them. They both stopped working. Isabel said something that made them both giggle. They started dabbing at their canvases again. Isabel appeared to speak to them for several more moments, then stood and continued on toward Bethany.

Isabel gestured toward Bethany's canvas and appeared to be complimenting her. Bethany looked happy and began talking animatedly. Isabel sipped her tea and looked as though she was listening intently.

"What is this?" said Kimberly "Damage control?"

Dulcie was in awe. "I think that's exactly what it is. The question that I have, though, is who instigated it? Was it her idea, or did Logan, or more likely Linda, suggest it?"

"That's a very good question. Shall I ask her?"

Dulcie looked, wide-eyed at Kimberly. "How could you pull that off? You can't just outright say, 'who put you up to this?' could you?"

"Oh, I have my ways!" she said mysteriously.

Isabel was approaching them. "Follow my lead," Kimberly whispered. "Good morning!" she called out to Isabel.

Isabel smiled radiantly. "Good morning to both of you."

Dulcie felt instantly dumpy. Isabel was like a tiny, golden doll. *'The British accent doesn't hurt, either,'* Dulcie thought. "Good morning," she replied aloud, trying desperately to mask her thoughts.

Suddenly, the wind howled. Kimberly grabbed her canvas. "We seem to have trying circumstances today!"

She laughed as she wrestled with it for a moment before clamping it down again. "There! All set. So how is the Dumbarton household getting on this morning?" she didn't look at Isabel as she spoke. Instead she busied herself with her paints.

"Oh, we're fine. A bit slow as always," Isabel replied.

Kimberly chuckled. "I do know that, ever since I've been retired! Are you usually the first one up, or is it the ever efficient Linda?"

A shadow came across Isabel's face. She quickly gulped her tea. "Usually it's Linda. This morning, I woke up early, though. It must have been the wind. It seems to make everyone angry." She took another mouthful of tea, as if stopping herself from saying too much.

Dulcie thought she could see where Kimberly was going with the conversation. "You're right," she said. "I barely slept at all last night with the wind howling. My brother runs a tour boat, and he never goes out on days like this." She turned to the house. "Is Logan up and about? Will he be doing a critique today?"

Again the shadow came over Isabel. "Yes, he'll be out later. I think I'll join him too, if that's all right with you. I've wanted to learn more about his work, so this would be a good way for me to do just that without taking up any of his time, really."

Kimberly nodded her agreement. "He seemed distraught during his critique yesterday. Has he been working hard lately?"

Dulcie held her breath. It was a more direct question than she would have dared ask.

Isabel turned and gazed across the water. "Yes. He's pushing himself in a new direction. Linda has scheduled quite a number of showings as well." She started to take a drink of tea, but realized her cup was now empty. "I am…, I think…," she looked confused. "I'd best get more tea. Cheers!" She raised her empty mug to them and attempted a happy look but failed. Quickly, she retreated back into the house.

"Well, what do you think?" asked Kimberly.

"I think that she is one unhappy woman. I also think it's her idea to do damage control. Linda would only make excuses for Logan. Or ignore his behavior. I don't think Isabel has any interest at all in Logan's painting. She wants to make sure that he behaves."

"I'd pretty much concur on all counts," replied Kimberly.

☃

Thursday's windy weather brought in pouring rain overnight, along with an oppressive heat wave on Friday. Willow was the first to arrive at the Dumbarton's rented house. She was hesitant to get out of her car and set up on the lawn. She waited for as long as she thought she could, then slowly gathered her items from the back seat. *Why did I get here so early?'* she thought. Looking at her watch, she realized that she wasn't early at all. The others were all late.

Willow trudged up to the lawn and began to set up. Suddenly, she sensed someone nearby. She turned quickly and nearly gasped, then stopped herself. It was only Isabel. She held out a cup of tea. "I don't know how you like it, but I just took a guess and put in a little sugar," she said.

"That's exactly how I like it," Willow said. "Thank you!" First Bryce, and now Isabel. Why were people suddenly being nice to her? She surreptitiously looked at Isabel over the top of the mug as she drank. She was so exotic. Beautiful, intriguing, and strangely magnetic.

"Look, I know Logan's been dreadful. You really must ignore him. I mean, I know that he's here to give instruction so I suppose that's important, but try to ignore the rest." She glanced back at the house. "That's what I certainly try to do."

Without thinking, Isabel reached out and stroked Willow's arm. Her skin was as soft as she had thought it would be, in spite of being covered with tattoos. "I know what it's like," she said quietly. "To have someone yell at you. And use you."

Willow froze, but did nothing to stop Isabel. Willow just watched her delicate hand gently stroking her arm. The glittering rings with stones of so many colors flashed in the morning sunlight. Willow felt as though she was in a trance.

A car drove up. Willow's head snapped around toward the driveway and Isabel dropped her arm. Bryce got out, looked over at them, and jerked his chin up in his typical, *I'm too cool to wave'* greeting. As he did, Isabel saw the curtains of the house move. Without turning her head, she cast her eyes to the window. Linda was staring at her.

Isabel finished her tea in one, long drink. She looked at Willow's cup. It was nearly empty. "Shall I take that?" she asked. It was a statement, not a question. Willow silently handed it to her and, as Bryce walked across the lawn to join them, Isabel hurried back into the house.

"What, did I scare her off?" he said with surprise. He was usually more successful with women.

"Someone did," Willow replied. She had seen the curtains flutter closed.

Bryce looked back and forth between her and the house. Then he shrugged his shoulders and continued on to his usual spot.

As the other students arrived and set up, the temperature continued to rise. Bethany brought her usual cooler and let the others put in their drinks. A lively discussion took place regarding the effect of heat on oil paint. As an art instructor, Scott stepped in to resolve the question. "Usually the hot weather makes the paints dry more quickly, so you either need to use more paint on the canvas, or..."

"Make it fatter," a voice booming with arrogance said from behind them. The group had been facing toward the ocean, looking at Scott's painting. They turned *en masse* to face Logan Dumbarton. He looked down his long nose at Scott. "Never use more paint than you would normally. Add linseed oil to extended the drying time. Besides," he scanned the group with disdain, "I don't think that any of you can afford to use additional paint." He chuckled his condescending laugh.

No one knew how to respond. Scott looked angry and frustrated at the same time. He felt that he had to say something. "Don't you think that you should restrict your comments to art instruction rather than handing out an analysis of our lives?" he asked in a low, even voice.

Logan took one step toward him but did not deign to look at him. "No," he replied.

Everyone looked at each other. No one dared look at Logan. Kimberly cleared her throat. "Well, I for one have plenty of paint *and* plenty of linseed oil today, so I'll try both methods and report back to all of you!" she said, attempting a light tone. She heard Logan snort quietly and caught the sneer that crossed his face. Scott smiled at her. It was a smile that said, *'Thank you!'* Before Logan could speak again the students scattered back to their canvases and resumed working.

Although she had not heard what was said, Isabel had witnessed the scene from the house. She was heading toward the door when Linda spoke. "Rescuing them?" she asked innocently.

Isabel knew that her words were anything but innocent. "No, Linda," she said quietly. "I'm rescuing you. Without him, you are nothing." With that, she quickly left.

∛

The official reception for Logan Dumbarton was scheduled to begin in half an hour. Dulcie had double-checked the catering menu and had made sure that plenty of ice was on hand. The heat wave had not yet let up. As she looked at the mounds of ice, she suppressed the urge to jump in them.

"The Widow is hiding out in her usual spot!" Rachel whispered as she walked by.

"Thank you!" Dulcie whispered back. She did not have a good feeling about the evening. Her trust in Logan Dumbarton had been diminishing rapidly with each new day. The entire situation with him had become increasingly strained. Celebrating his presence at the museum, not to mention introducing him to board members and wealthy donors, seemed like a recipe for disaster.

Dulcie had asked Linda to make sure that he arrived on time at seven o'clock. Linda had responded, in her usual flat manner, that she would do her best but had no control over her brother. *'Really?'* Dulcie thought. *'You control his entire life. Or have up to this point.'*

The time went by quickly and soon guests were trickling in the door. Dulcie recognized several of the master class students. She was surprised to see Willow appear wearing a flowing organza dress. Her nose spike had been replaced by a small gold ring, and her tattoos were concealed by lacy sleeves. Dulcie smiled across the room at her, and she thought that Willow attempted the same. It came across more as disgusted look, but Dulcie decided to be charitable and assume that it was a smile.

At seven-thirty the guest of honor arrived. He appeared as he had when Dulcie had first met him, arrogant and suave. He wore a white silk shirt, with several buttons open, stone colored chinos, and very expensive looking tan leather shoes. *'Italian,'* thought Dulcie, *'and most certainly bespoke, hand-made.'* His blond hair was swept back from his face with just the right amount of gel. One lock fell artfully out of place. He accepted the glass of champagne that was pressed into this hand with a gleaming smile, but Dulcie saw him immediately whisper to his sister and shove it at her. It slopped on the front of her blouse. He did not apologize. Linda disappeared, then quickly reappeared holding what looked like a gin and tonic.

Isabel was at his side in complete contrast. Her glossy dark hair was braided down her back. She wore a deep purple sari with golden threads gleaming in the low lights from the gallery. She sipped her champagne while haughtily, with heavily mascaraed lashes, eyeing anyone brave enough to come near.

Dulcie patted the neat chignon that she had managed to achieve with her own chestnut-brown hair and approached them. "It's such a pleasure to see you," she lied. "You both look wonderful!" At least that wasn't a lie. She hoped that her enthusiasm made up for her lack of sincerity.

"Oh, but it is you who looks wonderful," replied Logan. "Along with my ever-beautiful wife of course!" he added with the annoying, self-deprecating laugh. Isabel did not even smile.

"There are several people here who are looking forward to meeting you," Dulcie said, glancing around the room. She spied the museum's wealthiest donor nearby. "If you don't mind?" she continued.

Logan heaved a great sigh. "Yes, of course," he replied flatly. Dulcie saw him catch Linda's eye. He jangled the ice in his now empty glass. Linda nodded and scurried away.

'I'm about to introduce you to yet another patron of the arts who would be more than happy to give you tens of thousands for what I'm increasingly seeing as the worthless crap that you create, and you consider it a chore?' thought Dulcie. She considered skipping the current introduction until Logan seemed to be in a better mood, but then remembered how much this particular patron had donated during the museum's last fundraising campaign. *'No, this is my job. Just take it on the chin,'* she thought unhappily. She forced a smile and made the introduction.

For the next hour Dulcie continued to circulate with Logan. She smiled, chatted, and attempted to conceal his often blatant condescending remarks. She never enjoyed any of these gatherings, even when the guest of honor was far more enthusiastic than Logan. This was always the worst part of her job as far as she was concerned. It all seemed so affected. But she knew it was necessary. She slid away from the current conversation in search of the next person on her mental list of those who should meet the famous artist.

As she scanned the room, Dulcie saw Linda slumped back against a wall near the coatroom. At that moment, Dulcie felt sorry for her. Linda would never be in the limelight. She would never get the recognition or accolades that she probably deserved. Dulcie shook her head. It was sad, really. Dulcie certainly did not like her, but she could respect how hard Linda seemed to work.

As Dulcie looked over at her, Linda suddenly changed. She stood up straight, her eyes wide. She was looking into the coatroom. Dulcie could not see into the room, so she had no idea what Linda was watching. It was certainly startling her, though.

Linda quickly turned away and edged across the room, quietly moving between the groups of people. At that moment Dulcie looked back at the coatroom and saw Isabel and Willow emerge. They did not speak to, or even acknowledge, one other, but as they were about to move in opposite directions, Dulcie saw Isabel put her hand on Willows bottom and subtly squeeze it.

"Wow!" Dulcie said out loud.

"Pardon?" a voice next to her replied. She had not realized that Kimberly was now beside her.

Dulcie quickly took a drink of champagne to mask her surprise at the scene she'd just witnessed. She swallowed hard and searched for something to say. "I'm thrilled that this many people were able to come!"

Kimberly looked around the room. "Is this unusual? I've been to a few openings and it seems as though they drew pretty good crowds."

"True," said Dulcie. "But we haven't had many artist's receptions so I really didn't know what to expect."

"Then I think it's a sign of success! Good for you!" Kimberly smiled.

Dulcie was still trying to process what she had seen. She excused herself from the conversation when the twins, Tara and Mary, came over to chat. Dulcie decided to retreat to her office for a few moments to collect her thoughts.

She was there for no longer than two minutes when Linda tapped on the door. "We're leaving," she announced dully.

"*What?*" exclaimed Dulcie. They were barely half-way through the reception. Dulcie knew of several people who would not be arriving until the final hour, but who specifically wanted to meet Logan Dumbarton. They were very good supporters of the museum and Dulcie did not want to let them down.

"Logan isn't feeling well. He wants to lie down. We're leaving." Linda's voice was flatter than usual. She looked very pale.

There was nothing that Dulcie could do. She could not force them to stay. She simply nodded and followed Linda out into the main gallery of the museum.

Logan and Isabel were already heading toward the front doors, but Dulcie was not about to let them make a show of leaving early. Instead she whispered "Security measures!" to Linda and pointed them in the opposite direction. Fortunately, Linda believed her and they quietly left through the staff door.

As she returned to the reception, Bryce sidled up. "So our illustrious guest and his entourage have departed? Big surprise."

Dulcie eyed him. He had on black jeans and a black t-shirt. Fortunately, this one had nothing printed on it. Dulcie had not made up her mind about Bryce yet, but decided that she did not dislike him. "Yes," she said with a deep breath. "Evidently Mr. Dumbarton was not feeling well."

"I can tell you exactly what he was feeling. He was feeling like he needed another gin and tonic, and you don't have any here. I saw his sister mixing the one he had from a cooler she had stashed in the coatroom. You just have this champagne, which is actually not bad considering that it's domestic sparkling wine and not really champagne. But I guess that wouldn't have suited Logan the Great anyway."

Dulcie was surprised that he knew about the sparkling wine. She had asked all of the bartenders to keep the bottles inconspicuously wrapped with cloth napkins. Perhaps Bryce was more refined than he was willing to appear? "You're right about the pseudo-champagne, Bryce, but please don't spread it around, if you don't mind. We've had to be a bit conservative lately."

"You've had to conserve a lot, I'd be willing to bet, considering where he's living right now, not to mention the paints that he uses. Man, they're freakin' expensive! I'm sure you're getting stiffed with the whole bill. Our fee for the class was steep for sure, but it's not nearly enough to cover what I've seen."

Dulcie had no idea the situation was so transparent. She could think of nothing to say.

Bryce shook his head quickly. "Don't worry. I don't think anyone else knows. I'm just very observant, and I'm good at putting two and two together." He winked at her and moved away.

Dulcie still wasn't sure if she liked him.

As the evening began to wind down Dulcie circulated through the room making apologies for the departed guest of honor. She tried to keep her own feelings in check, yet with every passing minute she felt herself become more angry. Finally the last group departed. Dulcie scanned the room. Only Kimberly remained. She waved Dulcie over.

"I don't want to overstay my welcome, I just wanted to get you alone for a minute," Kimberly said. "You asked me to be your eyes and ears, but I don't have much to report, especially with Logan & Co. leaving so soon."

Dulcie rolled her eyes. "Yes. Not the most successful of evenings."

Kimberly put a reassuring hand on Dulcie's shoulder. "I think everyone here had a pretty good time, so no worries there. I really didn't see much of anything happening other than Bryce cozying up to Willow and leaving with her just after Logan left. I've noticed them in class. There may be a budding relationship? But that's just me being a nosey Nellie."

Dulcie tried to hide her surprise. Evidently Willow had interests in both directions. Perhaps Bryce would keep her busy, however, and away from Isabel. Dulcie could only hope. The last thing that she needed at this point was a sordid love triangle to complicate matters even further.

"Good to know! Thanks Kimberly," Dulcie said.

"I also wonder…" Kimberly stopped.

"Yes?" Dulcie prompted.

"Logan's sister, Linda. She seems so strange. She stares at Isabel in an odd way. Linda takes her orders from both of them, so you'd think she would be seething with the addition of Isabel, but the way she looks at the girl, well, it just doesn't seem like anger.

It's more like she's looking at a puzzle, trying to work it out somehow."

"I know, Kimberly. The whole situation seems strange. I'm sorry that all of you in the class have had to deal with this. I'm considering cancelling the rest of the sessions and just sending everyone a refund."

Kimberly looked surprised. "No, you couldn't!" she exclaimed.

"Why do you say that?" Dulcie asked.

Kimberly laughed. "What I mean is, this is the most entertaining thing that I've done in a long time! An eccentric famous artist acting like, well, an eccentric famous artist! I've never seen that first-hand. The others agree with me. And not only is it fodder for cocktail party conversation well into the future, we all are actually learning something with each class session. Plus, the kids that are still in school will have this experience to put on their resumes, as they've mentioned. It's a big feather in their caps to list 'Master Class with Logan Dumbarton'."

Dulcie considered for a few moments. "You're right, Kimberly. I'll still talk with the other students again, just to make sure that they're comfortable with everything, but I won't cancel the class. For now, anyway. But if it gets worse…"

"We'll all come knocking at your door! Really, though, it's simply good entertainment at this point. And as I said, we are all learning something. He has given us some good tips, in between the put-downs."

"I just hope they're more than the tips you can read in a book," said Dulcie, still unconvinced.

"Truly, they are." Kimberly slipped on her bright pink silk jacket and patted her hair. "I'll still keep watch and let you know what I find out. I have to say, getting this little assignment from you has been a lot of fun already!" She grinned at Dulcie and wished her a good night.

Dulcie returned to her office, closed the door, and threw herself into her chair. "I'm glad someone's having fun with all of this," she announced. "Because I sure as hell am not!"

 C3

The next morning Dulcie decided to stop in at the Dumbarton house, ostensibly to check on Logan and see if he was feeling any better. She drove over at about ten o'clock assuming that the hour was late enough so that everyone would most likely be out of bed and at least starting their day. Dulcie knocked on the door but no one answered. The house was silent although the cars were in the drive. *'Maybe they're out by the water?'* thought Dulcie.

Glancing out toward the front lawn, Dulcie noticed a small figure curled up on the chaise. It looked like Isabel. Dulcie quietly walked out to her.

Isabel was wrapped in a blanket and staring out at the ocean. She looked slowly up at Dulcie. She gasped. Isabel had a very large, very fresh black eye.

"Isabel! What is this! What happened?" Dulcie exclaimed.

"I fell," she replied simply and looked back at the ocean.

Dulcie cleared her throat. "Isabel, truly are you all right? You should see a doctor…"

"I'm fine. I fell," she interrupted, this time without looking up.

Dulcie waited, but Isabel had nothing more to add. "Where are the others?" Dulcie asked.

"Still asleep, I expect. I don't know. I got up earlier than them. That's when I fell." She was certainly insistent.

Dulcie had no idea what to do or say. "All right. I hope you're better soon. Could you tell Logan that I stopped by to see how he was feeling?"

Isabel looked confused. "Feeling?" she said.

"Yes. Linda told me that he wasn't well last night. That's why all of you left early."

"Oh, right. That's what she told you."

Dulcie was feeling more confused and awkward by the second. She thought she saw movement inside the house, but decided that it was not the best time to speak with anyone. She began to walk toward her car, but turned as soon as she was within earshot of the house. "You should put some ice on that," she called out to Isabel. Dulcie wanted them all to know that she was aware of things being very amiss.

03

The master class students had set up in their usual spots on the lawn of Logan Dumbarton's rented house. A damp, chilly breeze swept in from the ocean. Most of the students wore jackets. Bryce's sweatshirt read: "*If it ain't broke…*" Dulcie noticed him positioned slightly differently; he could now easily see Willow.

Logan Dumbarton had not yet made an appearance. Dulcie saw movement in the house, but decided against knocking on the door. She certainly did not want to encounter a scene like she had the day before with Isabel.

Dulcie wandered over to Kimberly. "Any sign of anyone?" she asked quietly.

"Nope," Kimberly replied. "I was the first one here, too. I don't think anyone has come out of the house."

Dulcie nodded. Ten minutes passed, then fifteen. After twenty minutes Dulcie was getting annoyed. Really, this tardiness was intolerable! She felt that she had to see what was holding him up, and get him outside. She marched toward the door and knocked loudly.

Silence. Then a scurrying sound. The knob turned and Isabel stared at her, wide-eyed. Her bruise still looked horrible.

"Isabel, could I see Logan please? The class has already started and the students need his critique."

Isabel stood in the doorway. She seemed frozen. Dulcie heard Linda's voice in the next room. "Dammit, what is *wrong* with you this time?" She heard a loud slap. Dulcie pushed by Isabel and quickly walked into the house. She saw Linda standing over her brother. He was lying on the couch, motionless, wearing only a bathrobe.

Linda began to look frantic. She turned to Dulcie. "He isn't waking up! I shook him! I slapped him on the cheek! He isn't waking up!"

Dulcie quickly yelled, "Call 911!" to Isabel. The girl had begun to cry. Linda just stared at Dulcie. Now angry with both of them, Dulcie reached into her pocket, pulled out her cell phone, and dialed.

Logan Dumbarton was not breathing. By the time the paramedics arrived he had begun to turn blue. Dulcie had called out to the class on the lawn asking if anyone knew CPR. To her surprise, Kimberly said that she had been a nurse. She had rushed in and begun chest compressions. The other students had simply watched in horror.

As the ambulance pulled away, Dulcie realized that Isabel had disappeared. Linda had gone with her brother, but Logan's wife was not in the house. Dulcie turned to the group of students who now seemed to be in a collective state of disbelief. "I'm going to make some very strong coffee. I want all of you to have a cup if you like, pack up your things, and head home. I'll be in touch with everyone and let you know Logan's status." She had a feeling she already knew Logan's status. He would not be continuing with the class. Or anything else for that matter.

A few gulped down coffee and they all left quickly. Dulcie looked around the house for Isabel but there was no sign. She heard someone in the kitchen. Hoping that it was her, Dulcie quickly went back, but found only Kimberly washing out coffee mugs. She looked up at Dulcie. "When I called this situation *good entertainment* I certainly didn't have *that* in mind!"

Dulcie leaned against the counter and put her head down on it. She groaned and looked back at Kimberly "Do you think..., he's... um... "

"Yeah, he's dead," she said.

Dulcie closed her eyes. "Do you *really* think so?" she asked.

Kimberly turned off the faucet and wiped the last mug dry. "Dulcie, I knew he was dead when I was doing CPR. It was mostly just a show for the other students. The paramedics knew too, but they'll always try to revive someone. Most of what they were doing was just routine, though."

"What do I do now?" Dulcie said out loud, not even expecting an answer. Her mind was spinning.

"Now you wait for the autopsy. Then you help Linda and Isabel get themselves, and him, home. The rest is up to them."

Dulcie nodded. "Yes, you're right. I am concerned about Isabel, though. I can't locate her. I don't know if it was the shock, or maybe she didn't want anyone to see her eye."

"Her eye?" Kimberly asked.

"This just gets more and more weird, Kimberly. I came over here yesterday morning to check on Logan. That was the excuse I made, anyway. But no one seemed to be around. Then I saw Isabel on a chaise in the yard. When I went over to talk to her, she had a huge, fresh bruiser of a black eye."

Kimberly gasped. "How did *that* happen?" she asked.

"She said that she fell. That's all she would say," Dulcie replied. She felt her stomach turning over. The smell of turpentine had permeated the room from the studio nearby. The windows had all been closed. "The sooner they've all gone, the better," she said, more to herself than to Kimberly.

"Dulcie, you look awful. Let's go outside. I should get home, and you probably should too. Can I give you a lift anywhere?"

Dulcie shook her head. "Thanks, but I'll be all right. I'd better stop at the hospital first, then go back to the museum."

Kimberly rummaged through her purse and pulled out a card. "I'd like you to call me later today just so I know you're all right. Yes, I am being a mother hen here, but that's payment for my spying services." She smiled.

They walked out to their cars and Dulcie took a deep breath of the damp ocean breeze. "Yes, I will call you," said Dulcie. "This will all sort itself out, I'm sure." She was trying to convince herself more than anyone else but was, so far, unsuccessful.

I want to touch people
with my art.
I want them to say,
"He feels deeply,
he feels tenderly."
~ Vincent van Gogh

CHAPTER SIX

"Good to see you back," said Adam Johnson. "And I must say, you are always full of surprises!"

"Don't even start with me," replied Nick.

"Wasn't going to," said Adam lowering his large bulk into a rolling office chair. He'd been sitting in the same chair for years, and it was now a full six inches closer to the floor than the others.

"You need a new chair," said Nick.

"Don't change the subject," Johnson replied.

Nick sighed. It was inevitable. Might as well get it over with. "All right, gimme your best shot," he said.

Johnson walked his feet around on the floor in little side-steps, swiveling the chair to face his partner. "Naw, I can't give you a hard time about this one. You gotta be going through hell right now. Or you have been going through hell and this is getting you out of it. I just have one question: Why didn't you tell anyone?"

Nick considered for a moment. "Would you?" he finally said. "Here's what I've got: a family who hates me because I'm a cop and not a lawyer, and a wife who won't divorce me because she's holding out for my money. It's kind of embarrassing, wouldn't you say?"

"Yeah, I'd say," Johnson replied. "So that's why you didn't go for the little museum cutie?"

"Not how I'd describe Dr. Chambers, but yes, that's why."

They both sat in silence for a moment.

"So watcha been doin' these last few days away?" Johnson asked.

"If you really want to know, I've been, at last, extricating myself from the witch that I should never have married in the first place. I finally got evidence that's irrefutable grounds, so she can't string it out any longer."

"Why was she stringing it out? Wouldn't she get alimony or something if she divorced you?"

"All right. You might as well know all of it," Nick said wearily to his partner. "My family has a lot of money. I don't really. Ever since I left Boston and joined the force here, they pretty much cut me off. That was fine with me – I accepted it. However, there's a trust fund from my grandparents that I come into when I turn thirty."

Johnson's eyes widened. "And I happen to know that somebody has a birthday in the not too distant future!" he quipped as though talking to a five-year-old.

"Yes," Nick said, ignoring his tone. "She kept contesting the divorce, finding different reasons, just to string it along. If she could keep it from being final until after my birthday, she'd get half of the money."

"I'm guessing it's a pretty sizable sum," Johnson said.

"Yes," Nick said quietly. "It is."

"Well then, sounds like you struck gold almost literally, and not a moment too soon. I have to say I'm happy for you, Nick. I give you a hard time, but you're good at your job, and you're a good kid. World needs more folks like you."

Nick had been looking at the floor. He glanced up at his partner. "Thanks," he said.

"Don't mention it. Okay, pep talk over. I see ol' Tommy over there getting all heated up. Looks like he might have something to tell us," Johnson jerked his head in the direction of the office door. Nick swiveled around in his chair.

Officer Thomas Banks hurried across the room and handed Adam Johnson a report. "First report in on some guy who dropped this morning. Looks like turpentine poisoning. O.D. of some kind. They want you to look into foul play," he said breathlessly.

"Thank you Officer Banks," said Johnson decisively.

"If there's anything I can do to help out, to investigate something, I'd be happy to," he blurted out.

"Yep, we'll keep you in mind Tommy. Thanks much!" Johnson gave him a mock salute, trying to dismiss him.

Tommy looked dejected but left them with the report.

"That kid's eager. Too bad he doesn't have the brains to match," Johnson said.

"Yeah, I know. But he's good on a stake out. Never falls asleep at all, even without coffee. He's my first pick every time," Nick said.

Johnson was already reading through the notes. "Found unresponsive on couch at rented home... retired nurse nearby tried CPR... paramedics attempted to revive… DOA at hospital… Possible turpentine ingestion… heavy drinker."

"What'd he drink?" asked Nick.

"Whaddya mean?"

"Well, heavy drinkers usually have a go-to drink. Wonder what his was," Nick replied.

Johnson handed him the paper. Nick scanned it quickly. "Ah, here it is, I think. The sister was with him. She reported no regular meds that he took, but he had been drinking gin and tonics the night before." He continued reading. "Now this is interesting. Married, but only the sister was with him when paramedics arrived. The wife wasn't around, so no comment from her." Nick looked up. "I wonder if she knows yet?"

Johnson took the paper and looked at the address. "Cape Elizabeth. Nice place, right on the water, I'd think. Guess we better go check it out. You drivin'?" It was a rhetorical question. Nick always drove. Adam Johnson's car was perpetually full of junk. It took him a full five minutes just to clear off the passenger seat.

As they drove across the city Nick said, "I wonder why they said it was turpentine? G&T's are pretty common. They used to flavor gin with turpentine – that's what gin smells like to a lot of people. Wonder why they didn't think of that first?"

"Don't know. Does seem odd." They were silent until Nick pulled into the driveway of the house. It seemed very still as they walked around to the front and knocked. No answer. Nick reached down and turned the knob. The door opened easily.

From the first moment that they stepped inside, Nick knew why the report had listed turpentine. He could smell it. He walked through the house and found the studio. The canvas on the easel was still wet.

"Explains turpentine, doesn't it," said Johnson.

Nick nodded. He went into a small room behind the kitchen, what would normally be a pantry, and found a twin bed wedged in along with some clothes on a shelf. Johnson stood behind him. The room was so small that he could not fit in with Nick standing there too. "Man, this is ridiculous! Who would want to sleep in here? It's like a tomb!"

"Yeah, it does seem tight. I wonder if it was the sister? Maybe she didn't want to be in the way?"

They continued to look around. In the bedroom Nick found both men's and women's items. He noted there were more men's clothes. *'That's strange,'* he thought, *'usually it's the reverse.'* In the bathroom he saw only one toothbrush. He looked for the usual bathroom items that a woman would have — make-up, hair brush, face cream — they weren't there. "Hey Johnson, does this place have another bathroom?" Nick leaned over and stuck his head out of the doorway.

"Yeah, but just a half-bath. Over there," he pointed. Nick went in but didn't find any personal items. He went back to the bedroom and looked through the drawers. Nothing there either.

Nick yelled out to Johnson, "I think the wife's done a runner!"

Johnson was beside him faster than Nick would have expected. "You serious?"

"Yeah. Fewer women's clothes, no personal bathroom items."

"Points in that direction," said Johnson.

"Do we know what she looks like? Where's the sister right now?"

Johnson called in to the station. The sister was still at the hospital. "Get her to stay there. We need to talk to her," he said sternly.

Both men heard a car pull into the driveway. They looked out the window. "Well, I'll be," muttered Johnson.

Nick froze, speechless, as he watched Dulcie Chambers get out of her car.

Dulcie had seen Nick's car as she drove up to the house. She wasn't really surprised. It was an unusual death, so it would be fairly routine to have the police investigate. She had just hoped it would be different police, and not Nick. She slowly walked up to the house and knocked on the door.

Johnson opened it. "To what do we owe the honor of seeing you in these less than auspicious circumstances?" he asked. Dulcie rolled her eyes.

"Good to see you too, Adam. I wish we didn't have to meet like this. Again."

"Not the best way, that's for sure." He stepped back and let her into the room.

"Hi, Dulcie," Nick said. He was hoping that she couldn't hear his heart pounding from the adrenaline surge he had suffered after seeing her car pull up.

"Hi, Nick. Here we are again."

Silence.

Johnson cleared his throat. "All righty then! So Ms. Chambers, what brings you here?"

Dulcie put down her purse on the kitchen counter. "I'm responsible for Logan Dumbarton being here. He was a visiting artist at the museum. We had him teaching a master class, which met here," she gestured out toward the front yard, "just this morning. Unfortunately, Mr. Dumbarton couldn't make it."

Humor. It covered uneasiness, confusion, and fear. Nick had seen it many times. "Dulcie, I don't mean to be rude but we have to cut to the chase at the moment. Did you ever meet Logan Dumbarton's wife? We think she's run off and we need a description of her, vehicle information... anything that you can think of."

Dulcie looked surprised. "Of course. Yes, I've met her. She's petite, beautiful, golden skin, long black hair that she often wears pulled back, large brown eyes. She's British but I think she's originally from India. Oh, and she has a nasty black eye right now. I'm not sure what she might be driving. They rented cars and I didn't pay attention. I know she was in a green sedan last I saw her going somewhere. Rental car agencies would have the information. Probably his sister Linda made the arrangements so they could be in her name."

"Wait a second. Back up a little. A black eye? How do you know?" asked Johnson.

"I saw her yesterday when it looked very fresh, and again first thing this morning. She told me yesterday that she had fallen, but she looked very upset. I'm pretty sure she was lying."

"So she was here this morning. That's good. She probably hasn't gotten far. Thanks," Nick said quickly. He stepped into the other room and Dulcie could hear him talking on the phone. His voice sounded like a quick staccato.

Johnson seized the opportunity. He looked pointedly at Dulcie. "Go easy on him? He's been going through hell, and for some time I think."

Dulcie found herself annoyed. "I have nothing to '*go easy*' about, Adam. I assume you're implying that there was something between Nick and me, which there wasn't..." She stopped abruptly as Nick came back into the room.

Adam Johnson gave Dulcie a '*you know what I mean*' look. She sighed and nodded ever so slightly.

"They've got an alert out now," Nick said to his partner. "With some luck we'll track her down soon." He turned to Dulcie.

"What can you tell us about them?"

Dulcie took a deep breath. "Where should I start?" she said. They looked at her quizzically. She shook her head in dismay. "Okay, I'll start at the beginning of course, but this may take a while so get comfortable." She told them about the master class. She described Logan's dual personality behavior. She talked about his relationship with his downtrodden and unappreciated sister, as well as his very new marriage to a beautiful but evidently self-centered young woman. Finally she related Logan's condescending manner toward the students in the master class, and told them that Kimberly had been keeping her informed.

At last she stopped. "That's all I can think of for now," she added.

"Yeah, I'd say that's plenty," said Johnson.

Nick looked down at his notes. He had been scribbling madly while she talked. Dulcie knew that he had also recorded what she said on his cell phone, so she wondered why he wrote everything down also.

"You mentioned earlier that the wife had a black eye. Any thoughts on that?" Nick asked.

"No, none at all! It was very surprising! I just assumed that Logan had done it while he was in one of his moods. Or drunk. Or both."

"Don't think it really could have been an accident, like she said?" Johnson asked.

Dulcie shook her head. "I don't think so. It was the way she said it. *'I fell.'* It came out so quickly, and she repeated it. I really felt like she was covering something up."

"What about the sister?" asked Nick. "Could she have done it?"

"I don't see why. Plus, she doesn't really seem that strong physically." Dulcie thought for a moment. "No, I don't think she could have done it. I just don't see any reason."

Nick was still looking at his notes. He was trying not to look at Dulcie. Being in the same room with her was making him uncomfortable. He knew he had to talk with her, to explain everything about himself, his marriage, the impending divorce… but this investigation was the priority, unfortunately. "Anything else at all that you can think of right now?" he asked.

"No, that's it. I'll try to go back through everything when I get home this evening. Maybe something will pop back into my head. I'm sure I've missed some details."

"Completely understandable," Johnson replied. He said it in a fatherly, kind way that instantly put Dulcie more at ease. "We appreciate everything you've been able to give us so far."

"Should I call you if I think of something else?" The question was pointedly directed at Johnson. He looked over at his partner. "You can get in touch with either…" he began to say, but one look at Nick changed his answer. "Actually, I'm working on something until tomorrow afternoon, so better contact Nick first. You have his number?"

Did she have his number? Oh yes, in so many ways, she thought. Dulcie sighed. "Yes. Yes I do."

CS

Nick paced up and down his apartment floor. He stopped after several minutes and stared at his phone, willing it to ring. It did not. He began pacing again.

'Just talk to her,' he thought. *'She's a rational person. Just call her up.'* The thought terrified him. But he knew that he had to clear the air, and the sooner the better. Not only was the situation driving him insane, but he also had an investigation to continue.

He picked up his cell phone, found her in the contacts list, and punched the CALL button. He didn't realize he was holding his breath.

The ringing sound stopped. She had answered, but he heard only silence. Then, after what seemed like an endless pause, she said, "Hi, Nick."

Now he exhaled. He didn't know what to say. Somehow his mind hadn't gone past the calling part. He had not actually thought through the conversation. "Uh, hi Dulcie," he muttered. *'Oh, very good. Very suave,'* he thought. *'Get your act together!'* He inhaled again, audibly. "Could we get together and talk?" he asked. *'Okay, that was fine. Just open the door...'* he thought.

"About Logan Dumbarton, I assume?" Dulcie said pointedly. Annoyance had crept in to her voice.

Nick closed his eyes and scrunched up his face. She had every reason to be annoyed. "Yes, of course," he replied.

Dulcie was silent for a moment. At the very least, she had expected him to allude to their situation. *'But then again,'* she thought, *'I've already said to Adam Johnson, to Dan, to anyone who cared to listen, that there is no situation. There was nothing between us.'* She decided to give Nick the benefit of the doubt, for the moment. "I have some time right now. Have you had supper yet?"

Nick wasn't expecting that question. His stomach growled. He hadn't even had lunch. "No," he answered simply, and again berated himself for being completely unable to put together a coherent sentence.

"Good. If you bring over chicken fried rice and an egg roll in the next twenty minutes, I can talk."

"I can do that. Thanks, Dulcie." He hung up before he said anything stupid.

Dulcie paced around her living room for some time, trying to convince herself that she really did not need to know anything about his personal life. Her association with him was strictly business. It had to be. She went in the kitchen and poured a glass of wine. *'Damn it!'* she thought, looking at the label. *Why does this have to be one that I know is his favorite?'* She thought about opening another bottle, or better yet just gulping down the glass before he arrived. But then she heard a knock at the door. *'Too late,'* she thought.

She peeked through the curtain and saw him standing on the porch with a large take-out bag. She swung the door open far too quickly and it banged against her foot. "Ouch!" she winced. *'Good move, Dulcie. Very smooth,'* she admonished herself.

Nick let out a sigh of relief. At least she had done something clumsy first and not him. *'Good. That means she's nervous, too. At least it helps me a little,'* he thought. "You okay?" he asked.

She nodded and gestured for him to come in. She limped behind him to the kitchen. Without thinking, Nick reached into the cupboard and took out plates. He had been to her townhouse several times, and knew where she kept things in her kitchen. He hesitated, putting them on the counter.

"Yes, good idea," Dulcie said, deciding to ignore his familiarity. She grabbed the bag and brought it in to the dining room table. "Want some wine?" she asked, trying to sound casual.

"I'd love some," he answered quietly, bringing in the plates.

Dulcie brought out another glass and poured, then topped hers off. She dished out a healthy portion of chicken fried rice and, when he had served himself, started eating. They sat in silence for several moments.

Dulcie finished her rice, put down her chopsticks and took a sip of wine. She sat back in her chair. "So, you're married!" she said.

Nick closed his eyes. *'Here it comes,'* he thought, waiting. But Dulcie said nothing more. He opened his eyes again. "Do you want the short version or the long version?"

"What makes you think I want any version?"

"Because you brought it up?"

Well, he did have a point there, she thought. "Whichever version you're up to telling, I guess." Dulcie glanced at him. He looked horrible – very pale and twice his age. She hadn't noticed that before. "You certainly kept it a secret," she added softly.

Nick exhaled a long, slow breath. "I think that was mostly denial. I hated myself for letting it happen. It was pretty much over before it started, although I didn't know it. I did everything that my family wanted, including marry the *right person* according to them. I was the legacy of the family law firm, the family name. The problem was, I was completely miserable and hated every second of it. Not just the marriage, either. So I jumped ship and filed for a divorce. But it wasn't that easy."

Dulcie cocked her head sideways. "Why not?"

"Money. That's what it always comes down to, doesn't it? Money. I come into a trust fund when I turn thirty, which is only a few weeks away. Divorcing before that would give her very little alimony given my current wage. Divorcing after would mean that she would get half of a very large sum. So she's been contesting and stringing it along."

Dulcie nodded. "Will she get away with it?" she asked, now curious.

Nick chuckled in spite of himself. "No, that she won't. Not now. She slipped up with her indiscretions. I can close this entire situation very quickly, or so my lawyer tells me. I won't believe it until I have the final papers."

"That's smart. Nothing's ever a done deal until it's actually done." Dulcie found herself sympathizing with him and tried not to. "But I can't believe that you're completely a victim in this entire situation."

"No, I'm not. That's the worst part. I take full responsibility. I was stupid. Stupid and weak. I let everyone else decide what was right. Granted, as an only child my parents did have a lot of influence. And my soon-to-be-ex's family and mine had been friends since before either of us was born. If I'd been a stronger person, and more clear-headed, I would have stood up to them all from the start. But I just plodded along the path that they chose."

"What made you stop plodding?" Dulcie asked, "What woke you up?"

"I think it was facing the real world as opposed to school. I got married the day after I graduated from Harvard. Then I started law school a couple of months later. When I was done with that, I had to face being a lawyer, playing the game, and being a husband to someone that I didn't love. Heck, I didn't even *like* her at that point. I couldn't imagine sitting in an office, laboring over paperwork, then going home to someone that I essentially loathed. So I applied for a job in Portland and walked away. The rest you know."

"Yes," Dulcie said quietly. "The rest I know."

"Can I ask you, Dulcie," he leaned forward in his chair. "What now?"

She knew what he meant. Unfortunately, she did not have an answer to that particular question. "Now, we finish our supper and talk about Logan Dumbarton," she said decisively.

He sat back, looking as though he had been stung. Yes, he deserved that. He nodded, and they finished eating in silence.

When the dishes were cleared, Dulcie told Nick everything that she knew about Logan Dumbarton, his strange sister, and his newly acquired wife. As she talked, she realized just how odd the entire situation had become. "It's funny," she concluded, "when you're in the middle of it all, you roll with it and convince yourself that it's just a difficult situation. But when you're back on the outside looking in, you realize how strange it all is." She looked pointedly at Nick. "You really do think that there was something odd about his death, don't you."

He nodded. "Yes. He was a drinker, certainly, but too many other aspects don't add up. For example, why did Linda contact you initially? Why would they want to leave London and come over here to a small museum – sorry, I don't mean to be condescending in any way – when he most likely could have had plenty more shows in much larger venues? And why did his sister think that he would come alone, especially when he had just recently been married and, according to what you've told me, he couldn't even make himself breakfast without someone else's help."

"I wonder if Linda just needed a break?" mused Dulcie. "And maybe she thought that if she kept Isabel away, the marriage would fall apart? She didn't seem overjoyed to have a sister-in-law. Not that one, anyway."

"I don't like the fact that his wife has run off. She won't get far, especially with a British passport. If she tries to fly back to London, the authorities will stop her," Nick said.

"What about Canada?" asked Dulcie.

"We notified border crossings, just in case." Nick shook his head. "People only run for one of two reasons. It's either toward something or away from something. In this case I feel as though it's the latter, but I don't know why."

"Because of her black eye?" asked Dulcie.

"Precisely. From what you've said, he didn't seem like a wife beater. Arrogant, annoying, and even maybe overbearing but not the type to physically attack. Then again, when someone is provoked…"

"Or drunk," Dulcie added.

"Or provoked *and* drunk," said Nick.

They both looked down at the table, lost in thought. A foghorn sounded in the distance. The night had turned chilly and damp.

"Well, I should get going." Nick stood up. "Won't know anything else until the coroner's report."

"Unless Isabel turns up first," added Dulcie.

"I'm not putting my money on that one yet. Meanwhile, I need to talk to this sister of his."

"Yes, well good luck there," said Dulcie, now standing as well. "Prickly and evasive would describe her pretty well."

"Thanks. I'll keep that in mind. I'd also like to talk to the students in his class. They might have some insight. Could you get me their names and contact info?"

"I'll have it for you first thing tomorrow morning," said Dulcie. "But I'll warn you, none of them liked Logan Dumbarton."

Nick had been walking toward the door. He stopped and faced her. "Really? That's surprising. I would have thought that they signed up for the class because they admired his work on some level."

"I'm sure they all did, and perhaps some still do. But our dear, departed friend had a way of making enemies. I've never seen anyone fling the insults with quite so much aplomb as Logan Dumbarton. He basically belittled every person in that class."

"Enough for anyone to try and get even?" Nick asked.

"I wouldn't think so, although you never know. When some people are insulted, they can carry a severe grudge."

"Still, it seems pretty extreme to kill him if they've only known him for a week," Nick said.

"Very true, although maybe someone had known him for much longer?" Dulcie conjectured. They had reached the door. She opened it for him. "Thanks for dinner," she said.

"Any time," Nick said. "I mean that." He walked onto the porch. Dulcie turned on the outdoor light, although in the growing fog it only created an ethereal haze around them.

When Nick was half way down the front steps, he turned. "Dulcie, I'm sorry," he said.

She looked beyond him into the dark, misty street. "You have nothing to be sorry about," she replied, and closed the door firmly.

Art is never finished,
only abandoned.
~ Leonardo da Vinci

CHAPTER SEVEN

Willow woke up slowly. She knew that something was wrong. A feeling of dread had permeated her. In her groggy state she tried to remember if she had been in the midst of a bad dream. Then she opened her eyes and blinked several times.

Yes, now she remembered. It wasn't a dream. The horrible scene from the day before slipped slowly into her consciousness. She remembered Logan just lying there, with Kimberly trying to revive him. Willow had also known it was futile. She had seen a dead man before.

While everyone seemed to be in chaos for those few moments, Willow had looked for Isabel. She had finally spotted her. First, Isabel was standing in the bedroom doorway, staring blankly at her husband. Then, she disappeared into the shadows of the bedroom. When Willow saw her again, she was quietly slipping out the back door with a bag in her hand.

Willow knew she should have said something about it. Wives don't usually slip away when their husbands are dead. Yet, the look on Isabel's face, and the black eye that Willow had glimpsed, kept her silent.

She turned over in bed, away from the bright sunshine coming through the window. Why had she kissed Isabel? She had never done that before – kissed a woman. Everything about her was intriguing, mesmerizing. Kissing her was exhilarating and scary at the same time. Willow wasn't sure if she liked it, but it had been a thrill.

She picked up her head from the pillow and looked at the clock. Quarter past eight. Time to get up. She would have been out of the shower by now if she had been on her regular schedule and still attending the Logan Dumbarton Master Class. Now she assumed that the rest of the week would be free for her to do as she pleased. She had a job at a local warehouse tracking packages that were shipped in and out. They had given her time off for the class. At least she had a bit of a vacation now, although it certainly did not feel like one to her.

Her cell phone began buzzing. *'Who calls at this hour?'* she thought. *'And who calls me, anyway?'* She let it go to voicemail. Lifting herself from the bed, she padded barefoot into the kitchen to make coffee. She yawned widely and looked down at the phone on the counter. Two calls. She must have missed the first one. Maybe that's what had woken her up. She pushed the button on the coffee maker and picked up the phone.

The first message was from Bryce. "Hey, Willow. Just wanted to give you a heads up. The cops are probably gonna call you. They just called me and said they need to talk to all of us. Just routine, though, they said. It kinda caught me off guard, so I wanted to let you know in case... well, you know."

Willow knew. Everyone assumed from her rough exterior that she had some sort of unsavory, perhaps even criminal, background. They were wrong concerning the latter. Willow hated the interpretation, but when she looked at herself in the mirror, she couldn't help but admit that she would get that impression, too. The spike in her nose, the black lipstick, the tattoos... it was her wall that she had steadily built to keep everyone out. She had grown up in foster homes, none of which had been even remotely nurturing. Some were outright abusive. As soon as she was old enough, she had dropped out of school and supported herself.

Everyone kept their distance from her, which was exactly what she wanted. The only person who had ever shown her any caring was her mother, but she had died when Willow was only six years old. The memories were vague. Since then she had had no friends. No one that wanted her in their life. That was fine.

It was fine until the painting class. As an artist, Willow knew that she had some talent. She had entered juried shows and had her work displayed several times. She had even won a prize once. When she painted, she felt like a different person. After spotting the ad for the Logan Dumbarton Master Class she knew that she had to be a part of it. It was so expensive, but she had to do it. She thought that it could change her life.

It had, but not in ways that she had expected. Bryce had been kind to her, and even seemed interested in seeing her. She had bought that ridiculous outfit specifically for the reception at the museum, thinking that he would be more attracted to her if she looked a bit more feminine. Without her hard, exterior shell, however, she felt vulnerable. She was vulnerable. Maybe that's why she let Isabel kiss her. Willow had been a little drunk and Bryce hadn't paid much attention initially, so she assumed he wasn't interested. Her mind had been set in the direction of receiving some kind of affection, and after several drinks it didn't matter if it was Bryce or Isabel.

After the coatroom incident, Willow had begun to sober a bit. Bryce had made his way over to her and told her she looked pretty. He had talked with her about her painting. He seemed more interested in getting to know her than anyone had in the previous twenty years. She was flattered.

The coffee maker beeped that it was done. Willow poured coffee into her only mug and sat down in her ripped but comfortable armchair. Then she remembered the other call on the phone. She sighed, stood up, grabbed the phone, and sat back down again. Assuming it was the police as Bryce had said, she didn't really want to listen to the message. She took another sip of coffee and tapped the voicemail button.

Silence. Then someone clearing their throat. It sounded like a woman. "Willow?" It was a woman's voice. "Willow, it's Isabel. I'm scared. I took off from the house. I don't know what to do! I feel like I can trust you. Can you call me, please?" The message stopped.

Willow sat up quickly and spilled hot coffee on her bare leg. She inhaled sharply and wiped it off with her hand, then ran to the kitchen for a towel. While she dried off, she listened to the message again. Why would Isabel be scared? Was it that black eye? If Logan had done it, which Willow assumed was the case, why did Isabel run off? Why was Isabel calling *her*?

As she tried to decide what to do, the phone rang again. Willow froze, staring at it. The number was different from Isabel's. Willow answered.

"Is this Willow James?" a stern voice asked.

"Who's calling?" she said, not answering the question.

"Detective Adam Johnson, Portland Police," the voice barked.

"Oh, right. Yes, I'm Willow. What do you want?"

Johnson smiled to himself. He'd been told she was prickly. He could handle that type. "A few routine questions, that's all. We're just looking into the death of Logan Dumbarton, and talking to everyone at the scene."

Willow noticed that he hadn't added the words "of the crime" to the end of the sentence. That was good. Must have been natural causes, if you can call drinking yourself to death natural. She answered, "Sure. What do you need to know?"

"We'd like to speak to you in person, as soon as it's convenient. You can come to the station or I can meet you somewhere."

Willow shuddered. She had no intention of going into a police station. "I can meet you at Vicki's Diner. Would that work?"

"Absolutely. What time?"

Willow glanced at the clock again. Half-past eight. "How about ten o'clock?" That would give her some time to think, plus the diner would be fairly empty before the lunch rush.

"See you then," he said and hung up.

Willow put down the phone. *'He didn't even ask what I look like. How will he know...?'* Then she realized that she wouldn't be very difficult to find.

Linda had just been given permission to return to the rented house. She took a taxi from the hospital to Cape Elizabeth. *'This will go on my expenses for sure,'* she thought absentmindedly. Then she realized that she might not be able to charge the museum for expenses. She might not be able to collect any money from them at all.

She thought about the will. Logan had specifically asked her to change it so that Isabel got everything after the marriage. He had even called the lawyer himself to make sure that it had been done. Linda was very surprised. She didn't think that Logan even knew who his lawyer was.

What didn't surprise her was that Logan left it all to Isabel. Logan had never really considered his sister family. She was an employee. When he made money, she made money. She had never spent much of it, and had managed to accumulate a sufficient reserve for herself. Still, she fumed a bit about Isabel inheriting. Especially now, so soon. That did not seem fair at all.

The taxi pulled into the driveway. Linda paid him and gave him an insufficient tip. The driver swore at her just as she was out of earshot. Linda wouldn't have cared anyway. She went in the back door of the house and looked around her. They had been there, of course. The police. They would certainly have looked around. The death was still being investigated. The autopsy wasn't complete.

Linda was ready to leave. She never wanted to see this place again. She never wanted to smell turpentine again. She went into the studio and threw the windows open. An ocean gust blasted in and knocked one of the paintings off the easel. It fell face-up. Linda picked it up and suddenly felt a flood of anger wash over her. This was the abstract nude of Isabel. No one else would have known, as there was no female form apparent at all, but Linda knew. She knew about all of his paintings.

She stomped toward the window and was about to hurl it through when she had a better idea. Wasn't an artist's work always more valuable after they were dead? She looked at the painting. It was unmistakably his work, although it wasn't signed. No problem there. Linda found a small brush, squeezed out a bit of black paint, and carefully signed it as she had on many others.

When she had finished, Linda smiled at her work. Her reserve fund, she liked to call it. Logan had done many paintings that he deemed unacceptable. He would abandon them in his studio. Linda would then "clean up" for him. Then she would carefully sign them and store them away. Periodically she sold them without his knowledge. She thought about the stash that she had in a storage locker. Their value would probably be double now.

Linda went into the kitchen and picked up the large trash container. She brought it back into the studio and set it down with a thud. Then she proceeded to methodically pick up every item and toss it into the trash. When she got to the very expensive tubes of paint that Logan had insisted on having shipped overnight directly from France, she did not hesitate. Several had not even been opened, but in they went. Done. Over. Logan was gone. Goodbye to all of it.

She continued on through the house moving from one room to the next, picking up items, throwing away much more. She changed the bag in the trash can three times. When she reached the kitchen she went straight to the cabinet that held the gin. It contained three bottles of Bombay Sapphire, two of which were unopened. Linda dumped every last ounce into the sink. She turned on the water to wash it all down the drain and get rid of the smell. She hated gin. Then she threw the bottles into the trash and listened to them shatter.

Linda replaced the trash bag once again and went into the bedroom. That's when she remembered Isabel. The police had asked about the rental car. They had said something about locating Logan's wife. Linda looked in the closet and opened the dresser drawers. Logan's clothes were there, but very few of Isabel's. She looked in the bathroom. Isabel's things were gone.

Linda slowly left the bathroom and sat down on the bed. All of her actions up until then had been automatic. Clean up, pick up, throw away. She hadn't really thought about what came next. Isabel. What was she going to do about her? This was a problem.

She wasn't sure how long she had been sitting on the bed when she heard a car drive up. She pulled the curtain aside and saw Dulcie approaching the house. "Dammit," Linda cursed softly. "Just what I don't need right now."

Dulcie approached slowly, not sure if anyone was in the house. She knocked on the door.

After several moments, Linda answered looking distraught. Tears were in her eyes. She dabbed at them with a wadded tissue, then snuffled into it.

"Linda, I'm so sorry to hear about this. Is there anything I can do?"

Linda appeared to choke back a sob, then shook her head. "No, no. I have everything under control. I always have done that for Logan. He's relied on me, and...," she blew her nose again.

"I know this is hard. I lost a very dear friend recently. It's difficult to comprehend it. Can I get you anything?"

"No, thank you. Really, I'll be fine. I'm not sure where Isabel is, but I expect she'll be back soon."

Dulcie wasn't sure what to say. Should she tell Linda that her sister-in-law had apparently run away? Did she ask Linda if she had any idea where Isabel could have gone? "Yes," Dulcie replied. "I'm sure she will. Do you know where she went?" Dulcie asked. It was an innocent enough question. For all Linda knew, Dulcie could have been asking if Isabel went to the store.

"No, but as I said, I'm sure she'll be back soon." Linda attempted a smile while wiping her eyes. "I've just been cleaning up a bit here. We'll be heading back to London as soon as the autopsy is..." she choked back another sob.

"Yes. Well, please call me if you need anything," Dulcie said reassuringly. Linda didn't seem as though she wanted company.

Linda went to the back door and opened it. She sniffed loudly. "The only thing I can think of right now is a check for Logan's services. I'll get an invoice to you. Thank you for coming by." She wiped her nose again and held open the door.

Dulcie could not think of what to say. A check? At a time like this, Linda was thinking about a check? Dulcie simply nodded and left.

Linda closed the door behind her. She backed up several steps so that she could not be seen from the outside. She watched Dulcie pull her car out of the driveway and continue down the road. When she was gone Linda opened her balled up tissue and took out the small piece of raw onion that she'd managed to grab from the refrigerator before Dulcie had reached the house. Laughing out loud, Linda threw it in the trash can with everything else.

CB

"A check?" Dulcie's brother stood in front of her with both hands on his hips. He had stopped coiling the line beside him and let it drop on the deck in a tangled mess. "Her brother is dead, they don't even really know why, she's crying, and then she suddenly wants a check?"

Dulcie began to giggle. The strain of the entire situation was definitely getting to her. "I know! And I shouldn't laugh. It isn't right. But it does seem ridiculous!"

Dan sat down beside her. "I know it was her job to take care of business matters, but seriously!" He looked at Dulcie slyly. "Of course the question is, will she invoice the full amount, or just the time that he actually worked before he…"

"And, I think we're done here!" interrupted Dulcie, still giggling. She stopped. "That is a good question though. I'll just have to wait and see. I have to say, this entire scheme has been a disaster from the start, but I had no idea it would take this kind of turn." Her brow wrinkled as she thought. "It has been ridiculous in every sense of the word, but there's something else strange about it. I can't put my finger on it, but it just isn't right."

"I don't know, Dulcie. You might just be overreacting. It'll blow over." He leaned over, picked up the line again, and resumed coiling.

"You're probably right. But I did have to talk with Nick, unfortunately." She had tried to sound casual, but Dan knew better.

"And…"

"And nothing."

"I don't think so. You wouldn't have brought it up if it was nothing."

Dulcie huffed a big breath. "Fine. I had dinner with him last night. No, nothing major. It was suppertime anyway, so he just brought take-out over so he could find out about Logan and everyone else in the master class."

"That was it? That's all he did was eat and listen?"

"He was a perfect gentleman if that's what you mean."

"Nobody who comes on to my sister when they're still married is a perfect gentleman."

"Dan, he never made any moves on me whatsoever. He never asked me out. He was kind and understanding, and maybe he had an interest, but there was never anything untoward."

"Stop defending him. Just tell me what he said. I'm dying to know what an innocent he is."

Dulcie glared at her brother. Then her face softened. "You're right. I am defending him, and I shouldn't. The quick version of the story is that he had been groomed from the start for a career in law along with marriage to this woman evidently, and woke up to it all a little too late for some of the damage to have already been done. He jumped ship with the police job and has been trying to divorce her for a few years. She hung on because he's coming into some money very soon."

"Do you believe him?" Dan asked.

"Yes, I do. In every other way he's proven that he can be trusted. I mean, he's a detective, right?"

"And there's absolutely no corruption in the police force," Dan interjected.

"I know what you're saying. But yes, I do believe him and for the most part I trust him. I'm not going to be handing him my heart anytime soon, if that makes you feel better."

"Yes, it does," Dan said.

Dulcie stood up and started to coil another line. It was a natural motion for both of them, growing up with their father's fishing boat. They had both spent countless hours on the ocean. "What actually makes me believe him, and feel almost sympathetic, is his partner."

"That big guy? Johnson?"

"Yes," Dulcie laughed. "He is quite large. But he acts like a dad to Nick sometimes. He told me that I should go easy on Nick, that he's been through hell. Adam Johnson is as honest as the day is long. He wouldn't tell me that if it wasn't true." She cleated off the coiled line. "There, I've earned my keep."

Dan smiled. "Nice job! Almost as good as mine!" He ducked Dulcie's sideways swat at him. "I am glad that you're getting beyond that situation with Nick, though. Good not to let bad feelings fester. Now you and he can just go about your lives and if you bump into each other, it'll be fine and not awkward."

Dulcie hopped up onto the dock. "Right," she answered. "Absolutely no awkwardness whatsoever." She gave him a mock smile, then glanced up toward the museum. "Duty calls. I'd best get back to the office. I have an invoice to look forward to!" She smirked again.

Dan laughed and waved her off. He knew that Dulcie was doing exactly what she always did when the going got tough emotionally. She was distracting herself with work.

As Dulcie walked back up the dock toward the street she thought about her brother's words. *'Just go about your lives.'* Is that what she wanted? Did she want to go about hers and let Nick go about his, only bumping into each other from time to time?

og

Willow sat at the counter of Vicki's Diner stirring half & half into her coffee. Adam Johnson lumbered in and eased himself onto the stool next to her. She looked up at him and sloshed coffee over the side of the cup. "Dammit!" she said quietly.

Johnson handed her a napkin. The waitress came over and looked at him. "Usual?"

"Yep."

Willow watched the brief exchange. She wondered what Johnson's *'usual'* was. Within moments the waitress had brought over steaming black coffee and two raspberry danishes. She slid them in front of him. "Much obliged," he said. He jerked his head toward Willow. "Put hers on my tab."

"Will do, honey," said the waitress.

Willow snorted. Honey was the last name that she would have ever called Adam Johnson. He didn't appear to notice.

"So what do you want to know?" she asked him, suddenly feeling on edge.

"Whatever you want to tell me." He glanced down at her arms as she stirred her coffee. She was wearing a short-sleeved T-shirt and her tattoos were plainly visible. "Nice ink," he said.

She shot a wary look at him, thinking he was being snide, but saw him rolling up his sleeve. "Mine's not quite as good." An intricately worked dragon was wrapped around his forearm. "Misspent youth in California. Can't remember getting half of this. Pretty impressive though, huh?"

Willow smiled in spite of herself. "Actually, it is," she said.

Johnson sipped his coffee and took an immense bite of danish. He chewed thoughtfully, then asked, "So, you must be an artist?"

The wary look crossed Willow's face again. "Yeah, workin' on it."

"Don't work too hard. You're young enough still. Just go for it."

Willow was silent. She didn't know what to make of him.

Adam Johnson knew this. One of his great skills was the ability to either put people on edge or put them at ease. Both were useful. In this case it was the latter. In spite of his intimidating size and gruff manner, Willow was beginning to trust him.

"He was a jerk," she said suddenly.

"You mean Logan?"

"Yeah. He kept putting down everyone. Making them feel like they weren't good enough. It was weird. One day he'd be this sniveling whiner shuffling around, and the next he'd be an egocentric, arrogant ass. That's the one we all hated."

"Pretty strong emotions after just one week," said Johnson.

"You'd have felt the same if you'd been there," she replied.

"Anything else strike you as odd?"

Willow stared into her coffee. *'Not really,'* she thought, *'Just that his wife made out with me when I was drunk, then called me after he was dead while she was in hiding someplace and said she was scared.'* How much should she tell him?

Johnson knew she was holding back. He'd been doing this job for so long, he knew all the signs. "It's gonna come out eventually. You might as well tell me now," he said quietly.

"Tell you what?" she said defensively.

Now he swiveled his large bulk around on the stool to face her. "Like I said, either now or later. Your choice." He leaned over and reached around to his back pocket for his wallet. Willow couldn't believe that he'd finished both danishes so quickly.

She considered what he had said. Maybe she didn't need to tell him everything. Maybe she'd just tell him a little. After all, it didn't all have to come out. It wasn't relevant, surely.

"Fine. She called me."

"Who called you?" He appeared disinterested as he fished through his wallet for some cash.

"Isabel. She left a message for me this morning. She said she was scared and wanted to talk to me."

"Uh huh. Did you call her back?" He was getting up to leave now.

Why didn't he seem to care? "No," Willow answered. Now she was annoyed.

"Hmm. Let me know when you do. If she's in trouble, let me know that, too." He tossed his card on the counter in front of her.

"Fine!" Willow was nearly fuming.

As Johnson left he called out over his shoulder, "You're welcome for the coffee."

Once outside, Adam Johnson moved quickly. He got in his car and pulled out his phone. Nick answered after only one ring.

"Got something?"

"I think so. Just talked to that spikey girl. She said the wife called her this morning. Left a message that she was scared. Wanted Willow to call her back."

"Did she?"

"Nope."

"You're sure?"

"Yup."

"I'll get a dump from the cell phone tower so we can track the number Isabel called from. Maybe we're getting somewhere now." Nick said.

"Hope so," said Johnson. "I know there's more she wouldn't tell me. That's always a good sign. See you back at the station." He drove across the city as quickly as possible.

Willow finished her coffee. She picked up her phone, then put it back down. She fingered the card that Johnson had left on the counter. Impulsively she tore it in half. She was annoyed with him.

The feeling of dread that she'd woken with had returned. She put both halves of the card carefully in her pocket and picked up the phone again. Looking through the calls, she found the one from Isabel. Willow took a deep breath and pressed, "Call back."

"Honey, can you use that outside?" the waitress was now looming over Willow.

"Huh?" Willow hadn't heard her.

The matronly waitress gestured toward the door. Willow got the message. She got up and went outside just as Isabel answered.

"Willow! Is that you?" the voice was husky and quiet.

"Yes. Where are you? Why did you call me?"

"Look, I'm sorry to drag you in. I had to get away. I'm scared. I think I'm in really big trouble, and I didn't mean to do it!"

"What are you talking about? Do what?" asked Willow. She was confused.

"They think Logan was murdered, don't they? I did it, but I didn't mean to! I put turpentine in his drink! I didn't think it would kill him! I just wanted to make him sick so he'd stop drinking. He was so horrible when he drank! Oh God, what have I done?" Isabel's voice cracked. She was crying.

Willow couldn't speak for a moment as she tried to process everything that Isabel had just told her. "Listen, Isabel, the police are talking to everybody, but so far it seems like they're just following some routine. I haven't heard anything about murder!" Willow now believed that Isabel was truly insane. She was beginning to wish she had never signed up for this master class. "Where are you?" she asked again.

"Not far, actually," Isabel replied. "Look, I have to go. Can I call you later?"

"Uh, I guess so," Willow said.

"And don't tell anyone, please? I don't know what to do yet!"

"Look, I can't…"

"Please? Oh, Willow, I need your help! Please don't tell! I'll talk to you later!"

The phone clicked off. *'Great.'* Willow thought. *'And if he was murdered, am I an accessory now? Nope. No way am I going down with that.'* She rummaged in her pocket and pulled out the two halves of Johnson's card, held them together, then dialed.

"Yeah?" he answered quickly.

"This is Willow…"

"Yeah, I know."

"I need to talk. Should it be on the phone or do you want to see me in person?"

"Phone's fine. What's up?"

"I just talked to Isabel."

Adam Johnson sat up in his chair and waived furiously over to his partner seated opposite him at his own desk. Johnson gestured for Nick to listen. Nick hurried over and put his ear beside Johnson's.

"Great. Can you tell me what she said?"

Willow took a deep breath. "She said she killed Logan. But she didn't mean to. She put turpentine in his drink, but she only wanted to make him sick so he'd stop drinking. She said he was awful when he drank."

"Did she say where she was?"

"No, she only said she was nearby."

Nick breathed a sigh of relief. Johnson looked at him pointedly and put a finger up to his mouth to shush him. Nick rolled his eyes. "Anything else?" Johnson asked.

"Nothing that she said. But look, I'm only telling you all of this because I don't want to get in trouble. I feel like this is getting really ugly and I want out. I'm done. She called me, I called her, and now I've told you."

114

Nick knew that her response was rooted in fear, not anger. He nodded at Johnson. He knew it, too.

"Did she say she'd get in touch again?" asked Johnson.

Willow was silent.

"You there?" Johnson said.

"Yes," Willow's voice was very small. "And yes, she said she'd call again."

"Then we need you to hang in there with us, Willow. It'll all be fine, I promise. She's got nothing to be scared of, and neither do you. Want us to check in with you later today? Would that make you feel better?" Johnson was in his fatherly mode again.

Willow swallowed hard. Her face felt very hot and tears welled. "Yes," she said. Her voice sounded small. "I'd like that."

"Okay, no problem. Look, you go home and take it easy. I'll call in a couple of hours."

"Thanks," she said quietly. "Oh, and thanks for the coffee earlier, too."

"Don't mention it, kid," Johnson said kindly. He clicked off the phone.

Nick walked slowly back to his desk and sat down heavily. "They did say turpentine was suspected when they took him in," he said.

"Yeah, but we don't know anything yet. Autopsy report's not done. Let's not jump to conclusions."

"Why do I feel like we're chasing our tails?" asked Nick.

"Because we are?" Johnson replied. He looked at his watch. "Dammit, I gotta go meet the wife. She's dragged me into helping her pick out a baby shower present for our niece." He glanced over at his partner. "No comments from the peanut gallery!"

Nick was desperately trying to hide a grin. He could only imagine his partner poking through tiny baby clothes. "No comment at all! Are you taking her to lunch?"

Johnson hoisted himself from his chair and patted his backside to make sure he had his wallet. "Nope!" he said. "She's taking me! How do you think she got me to go in the first place?" He pushed his chair under the desk, gave his partner a half wave, and left.

Nick sat quietly for several minutes. He knew what he had to do next. He needed to talk with Dulcie. She had worked with all of these people. She had better insight than he would. He also knew that they would get nowhere with Willow and her contacts with Isabel. The only way to get Isabel to come out of hiding was to reassure her, and Willow was not exactly the reassuring type.

Dulcie. She was the solution. Somehow he had to get Isabel to talk to Dulcie. He knew he couldn't have Dulcie call her. Isabel would not answer. Unless... unless the call was from Willow's phone.

*Every artist dips his brush
in his own soul,
and paints his own nature
into his pictures.*
~ Henry Ward Beecher

CHAPTER EIGHT

Nick sat alone in Dulcie's office for several moments, then got up and went to the window. The sun was out, but he saw rainclouds in the distance. He turned back from the window toward the room. A nearby table caught his eye. There were several printouts of information on plants, along with vivid prints of different flowers. They looked like plates taken from a reference book. He was still looking at them when Dulcie came in.

"Hi Nick. Are you interested in botanicals?" she asked. She gestured toward the prints.

"Ah, that's what these are. You know, I've always liked them. I didn't know that they were considered actual art."

Dulcie nodded. "They're definitely on the spectrum. When people started drawing botanicals, it was mainly for identification. Plants were used for medicine, so it was pretty important to use the right one at the right time."

"I can imagine," Nick murmured still looking at the prints. "They look so fragile, it's amazing to think how powerful some could be."

"Definitely!" Dulcie said. *'Why did he have to say such thoughtful things?'* a voice inside her head asked. She blinked several times, trying to refocus. "I'm putting together a botanical exhibit. When I was in Bermuda I saw some beautiful paintings done by a woman about two hundred years ago. I'd had the idea for the exhibit already, but that was what really moved me along. I had such an interesting conversation there with a Bermudian who talked about her ancestors, and how people thought they were witches because they knew how to heal with plants. Funny how we just call them doctors now."

"Very true. I'll be interested to see the exhibit," Nick said. Dulcie always seemed to be doing something that intrigued him.

"I'm sure the next exhibit isn't what brings you here, though," Dulcie said as she went over to her desk.

"No, it doesn't. Can I close the door?" he asked.

She nodded, trying to ignore her rapidly increasing heartbeat. She inhaled deeply, slowly, uselessly willing herself not to blush.

Nick sat in the chair opposite her desk. "As you can imagine, it's about this Logan Dumbarton situation. There's a possibility that he was poisoned, but not intentionally. Well, it was intentional, but murder wasn't on the culprit's mind."

"That's enough to pique anyone's curiosity. Can you fill me in on a few more details? Such as, who this culprit might be?"

"Isabel Dumbarton."

Dulcie instantly sat back in her chair as though a force had driven her there. "If Isabel did it," she said firmly, "then it was completely justified."

"I don't follow you."

"She had a terrible black eye when I last saw her. It seems our famous artist was also a wife beater."

"I agree, that's reason enough to drive anyone to a pretty drastic act. But here's the problem. She's in hiding. We've confirmed that much. She's contacted Willow but won't tell her where she is. Willow told us that all Isabel would say is that she's nearby but frightened. Willow has also conveyed, in no uncertain terms, that she does not want to be an intermediary between the police and Isabel Dumbarton any longer. To be honest, I think Willow is scared too, although I don't know why. Logan Dumbarton is dead. He can't hurt anyone now."

"True. And I can see where this is going. You want me to be the intermediary and talk to Isabel."

"Yes," Nick said simply. "But we'll have to have Willow call her one more time with you there as well. I'm sure that Isabel won't answer if the call comes from anyone else's number."

"What about Linda? Certainly she knows Isabel much better."

Nick didn't have a good answer to this question. He was relying on his intuition, and it only failed him on rare occasions. He hoped this wasn't one of those times. "I have no good reason for saying this, but something tells me that she wouldn't talk to Linda."

Dulcie trusted Nick's instincts. *'Although that's the only thing I trust about him right now,'* she thought unhappily. "Tell me more about the poisoning. What did Isabel do?"

"This is all secondhand from Willow, so I don't know exactly. According to her, Isabel said that she didn't like the way Logan acted when he drank so heavily. She wanted him to stop, so she put turpentine in his gin & tonic to make him sick."

"Interesting. I just read about turpentine. Evidently in the seventeenth and eighteenth centuries, gin was flavored with turpentine instead of juniper berries because the turpentine was cheaper. After a few drinks, he might not have noticed the extra flavor." Dulcie looked thoughtful. "Here's what strikes me as odd, though. Turpentine, or its variations, has been used medicinally for a few hundred years. If my understanding of it is correct, it would take an awful lot to kill someone."

"We don't have the autopsy report yet, so we don't know if that really was what killed him," Nick said.

"So Isabel thinks she killed her husband, and she ran off and hid in a panic. Now she's afraid of the police, and doesn't know what to do. Never mind the fact that she's in a foreign country."

"Right, and that just complicates everything. So my idea is, I get you together with Willow, she calls Isabel, then hands the phone over to you."

"Okay, excellent plan so far, but what exactly do you want me to say?"

Nick stood and walked back over to the table of botanical prints. "I hadn't quite worked that out yet."

"If we find out whether or not the turpentine killed Logan, wouldn't that be a better time to talk with Isabel? I could at least tell her something conclusive, and with any luck she won't be a murderer."

"I'm not sure we can take that chance. If the turpentine did kill him, it will definitely be her fault and she may shut down contact altogether. I think it's better to try to coax her out while there's still the chance that she's innocent." He turned to look at Dulcie. "Could you play that up? The possibility that she's innocent? Maybe tell her what you just told me: it'd take a lot of turpentine to kill someone."

Dulcie was unsure. It was a difficult situation from any angle. She knew Isabel was vulnerable, though. Even if she was guilty, the fact that the death was unintentional and the fact that she was a battered wife would mean leniency from any judge. "All right. Tell me when and where," she said.

"How about here, and now. We need to do this as soon as possible. Let me call Willow. I told her we'd check in with her anyway."

Dulcie busied herself at her desk while Nick spoke quietly on his cell phone. When he was done, he quickly made another call. Dulcie heard him asking someone else to come to the museum. Now she was concerned.

"You're not bringing the entire police force over here are you?" she asked.

"Nope. That was just Johnson."

"Don't you think he would spook Willow? He can be a little intimidating, you know."

Nick smiled. He knew exactly what she meant. "Yes, he can. But oddly enough, he can be the fatherly type when he needs to be. He did that with Willow earlier and it worked very well. She trusts him, more than she trusts me, I think."

Trust. That word again. Dulcie didn't want to think about it.

Johnson arrived ten minutes later. He handed a report to Nick, and tipped an imaginary hat in greeting to Dulcie. Nick scanned the paper. "Seriously?" he said aloud, glancing at his partner.

"Yep," said Johnson.

"What?" asked Dulcie. "Anything you can tell me?"

"It seems that the car rented by the Dumbartons, the one that Isabel took off with, was returned to the rental agency. Or rather, it was parked in the lot, then a woman called them and said it was there."

"Was it at the airport? Would there be security cameras? Or taxi records of her getting a ride somewhere?"

"Nope. Unfortunately, it was left at one of their locations in the city, and in the outer section of the lot. They checked their cameras, but the video only shows a woman walking away."

"Well that's frustrating," Dulcie said.

Both men glanced up at her simultaneously. They each had the same thought. *You have no idea how frustrating this job is!* Johnson just looked to the heavens while Nick shook his head.

Rachel appeared in the doorway and tapped on it. "Knock, knock. You have a guest. Or I should say, *another* guest. This is quite a party in here!"

"I wish," quipped Dulcie.

Rachel stepped back and Willow came into the room. She stopped and glared at Nick and Dulcie. "This is the last thing I do here," she announced. "I don't like it, I didn't do anything, and I really don't want to see you people again. I'm done with this!"

"Absolutely," Johnson said.

Willow softened a little when she heard him speak. "You just want me to get Isabel on the phone, then I hand it to Dulcie, right?"

Johnson nodded. Willow pulled out her phone and started to call.

"Wait!" Dulcie exclaimed. "What do we want Isabel to do? Are we just initiating a conversation? Do I want her to tell me where she is? I haven't exactly done this kind of thing before," she said nervously.

"Ideally, we want as much as we can get. We want her to tell you where she is. We want her to stay there so we can pick her up. Make her feel comfortable. Make her feel like you understand and that she'll be okay. You want her to trust you," Nick said.

Dulcie nearly laughed at his unintentional irony, but she kept her thoughts to herself. She simply nodded.

Willow dialed. "It's ringing," she whispered. Then she said, "Isabel, it's Willow. I'm glad you answered. Are you okay?"

She put the phone on speaker mode. Everyone in the room tried to be as silent as possible. They could barely hear Isabel's voice. "Yes. I'm fine. Do you know anything more about Logan?"

"Isabel, I don't. But I know who does know something. Dulcie Chambers. Is it okay if I have her talk to you? I can't explain it very well."

Silence. They waited.

"Isabel?" Willow finally said, thinking that she had hung up.

"I'm here. Yes, I guess I'll talk to her. When?"

"Right now. She's right here. Okay?"

Again, silence. Nick mouthed *'Say something!'* to Dulcie.

"Hey, Isabel, it's Dulcie. I just wanted to tell you something that I know, and I think you'll feel a lot better," she hesitated.

"Go on," the small voice said.

"Isabel, it's really difficult to kill someone with turpentine, especially to poison them so quickly with it. I know you put it in his drink, but I'm pretty sure that isn't why he died." She stopped and held her breath.

Nothing. Again, they all thought that she had hung up.

"Do you know for sure?" she finally said.

"We don't have the final report on him yet, but I'm pretty certain," said Dulcie. "Isabel, I know you're scared, but I have an idea. Why don't you come stay with me while all of this gets sorted out? Would that make you feel better? You don't need to go back to that house again if you don't want to. I can come get you and bring you straight to my house. I live in Portland, very near the museum."

Now they heard muffled sobs. Her voice was choked. "Yes!" she managed to squeak in between them. "I've been so scared! If you think I'm not in any trouble... I'm scared to be alone!"

"Isabel, where are you? Where can I meet you?" Dulcie held her breath.

She hesitated for only a moment. "I'm not far from the house where we were staying. There's a shed that looked like it was abandoned near the beach. It's got a metal roof. If you go left on the beach when you come out of the house, you'll see it farther along."

"Don't move. We'll be there in twenty minutes!" Dulcie said as calmly as she could. "Do you want me to keep talking to you while I'm on my way?"

"No," said Isabel, "my phone battery is dying. I can't talk long. I should go." The phone clicked off.

"Let's go. Now!" said Nick, already heading for the door.

"Hey, can I get my phone back?" said Willow.

"Not yet!" Dulcie cried over her shoulder. "It's the one number that Isabel knows!"

"Well in that case," said Willow. She bolted after them.

Nick drove as quickly as possible to the house. As the car careened along the road, Dulcie thought, *Please let Linda be away. Please let her be away from the house!* The last thing that they needed right now was another complication. Her pleas went unanswered, however. When they pulled into the driveway, Linda's car was there.

Nick sprang out of the driver's seat and ran around the house. Dulcie was hard on his heels. They ran up the rocky beach, their feet crunching on pebbles. "There it is!" shouted Nick.

"Wait, let me go first!" Dulcie called from behind him. He slowed.

Dulcie ran past until she was nearly at the shed. She dropped her speed to a slow jog, then a quick walk. Panting, she reached the shed. "Isabel?" she called. "Isabel, it's me, Dulcie!"

Nothing. They heard only the waves crashing, one after another, with agonizing slowness. Then, the door swung open with a loud squeak. Isabel peeked out, took one look at Dulcie, and lunged toward her.

Nick was beside them in a second. For a moment, he thought that Dulcie might be in danger. Fear could make people do strange things. It could make them lash out at those trying to protect them. But Dulcie simply held on to Isabel tightly as her body wracked with sobs. She began to collapse onto the sand. Nick grabbed Isabel, taking her from Dulcie and holding her up. "You're safe! You'll be fine! You're safe!" Dulcie repeated over and over.

Linda had heard the commotion and saw all of them running around the house. With heaving breaths she came jogging up just behind Johnson, who was lumbering along as fast as his stumpy legs could move him.

"Isabel!" Linda gasped. "Where have you been? What on earth…?"

Nick felt Isabel's entire body stiffen when she heard Linda's exclamation. "No!" The voice in his ear didn't even sound real. It sounded like something that had blown through him from the ocean. "No!" he heard again. It was Isabel. "Don't let her near me!"

No one else could have heard her. He held her more tightly. "I won't," he said under his breath. He called out to the others, "We need to get her to a doctor! I think she's dehydrated." It was the first thing that popped into his head. "Johnson, help me get her to the car!"

Johnson jumped forward. He had worked with Nick for long enough to tell when he was up to something.

"No! Put her in the house! It's much closer! I can get her something to drink!"

"No ma'am. This lady needs a doctor. We'll be in touch and let you know her status," Johnson said, looming over Linda.

Linda began to protest again, but Johnson gave her his most intimidating look, and she closed her mouth. They reached the car, and Nick put Isabel carefully into the back seat. "I'm going with you!" said Linda firmly.

Dulcie got in next to Isabel, and Willow quickly jumped in on the other side. "No room!" Dulcie said. Nick had already started the car. Dulcie slammed the door and opened the window. "I'll call you later," she told Linda as the car backed out.

Linda stood by the house gaping at them as the car drove away.

СЗ

Nick sat at his desk in the police station pondering a blank computer screen. Johnson sat opposite him doing the same. Neither spoke for several moments. They had just returned from depositing Dulcie and Isabel at Dulcie's townhouse, then dropping off Willow at her apartment. She had seemed decidedly more confident, so both men assumed that she'd simply been spooked by Logan's death and Isabel's strange phone calls.

Nick realized that he badly wanted coffee. He stood and walked by his partner. "Get me one too?" Johnson asked.

"How do you know I wasn't just going to the bathroom?" Nick asked.

Johnson chuckled but said nothing.

Nick came back with the Office Swill, as they called it, and plunked one down in front of Johnson. "Much obliged," he said before sipping it and making a face.

Officer Thomas Banks scuttled rapidly into the room. "Hey, look you guys! That report you were waiting for! I've got it! Wanna see it?" He was waving a piece of paper in the air.

"Whoa there, Tommy! Don't burst an artery! Yeah, we'd love to see it!" Johnson said, trying to snatch it out of Tommy's rapidly moving hand. Nick stood up and calmly took it from him.

His eyes darted back and forth across the paper. "Well, Isabel Dumbarton is off the hook," he muttered at last. "Thanks, Tommy," he said, dismissing him. Tommy remained firmly planted in front of Nick, eyes wide like a puppy.

Johnson forced a stoic look. "I think we'll need to go check out that, uh, place that we talked about before, don't you?" He looked pointedly at Nick.

Nick caught on immediately. "You're right. Better get a move on."

"Can I come with you guys? I can keep watch if you need me to!" Tommy said hopefully.

Johnson stood and put a beefy hand on Tommy's shoulder. "What we really need is somebody to be here at the station in case there's an update. Can you do that for us?" He looked solemnly at Tommy.

"Oh yeah! Sure! No problem! Want me to call you if something comes up?"

"Absolutely, Tommy! That'd be perfect!"

Tommy was grinning as the two detectives left the station.

"You know nothing is going to come up," said Nick.

"Yeah, but he doesn't. He'll be high on the anticipation for the next two hours. Then his shift'll be over anyway."

Nick shook his head. "I feel bad for the kid. He'll never make detective."

"Hope springs eternal," said Johnson. He looked at the report that Nick was holding. "So what's happening?" he asked.

"Let's get a real coffee and you can read it," Nick said. They had been subconsciously following the brick sidewalk toward Roasters since leaving the station. It was their second office.

Nick handed off the report to his partner who took it and sat in a booth. Johnson didn't trust the delicate metal chairs at the café tables. Nick came back with two steaming paper cups. He waited for Johnson to finish reading.

"Huh! Okay, so it looks like it was heart failure. Turpentine wouldn't cause that. Renal failure, yes, especially for a heavy drinker. But prob'ly not the heart."

"Right," Nick said as he sipped his coffee slowly.

"So open and shut case. No funny business," Johnson said, handing him back the paper.

"Right." Nick dragged the word out slowly, without much enthusiasm.

Johnson watched his partner as he stared out the window.

"That was somewhat less than convincing. You know something I don't?" Johnson asked.

Nick put down his coffee. "No. No I don't. It just doesn't *seem* right."

"What doesn't seem right? The wife ran off because she thought she'd poisoned the hubby and killed him. She had a bruiser to justify it. But turns out he died of natural causes. Case closed."

"I don't know," said Nick. Something was niggling at him. It frustrated him. "Yes, I agree. On the surface it looks pretty straightforward. But something was happening out on the beach when we found Isabel. Something doesn't sit well with all of this."

"Any thoughts as to what *exactly* this *something* might be?"

"Nope. The only thing I can say is that Isabel did not want to see her sister-in-law."

"Well I'm sure there's no love lost there, if I have all my facts straight."

Nick nodded. "Just doesn't feel right though." He looked at his watch. "Let's keep this case open for another day or so, just to let everything settle. Nothing else is pressing right now anyway."

"Sure, I can do that," Johnson said. He knew his partner well enough to trust his instincts.

"I'm going to take a walk. See if I can jar any logic out of this brain," Nick said pretending to punch his head as he slid out of the booth.

Johnson laughed. "Yeah, good luck with that. See you tomorrow." He sat back comfortably in the booth, his eyes straying toward the pastry display.

Nick stepped out on the street. A light rain was beginning to fall. He had always liked the rain. It seemed to make everything more quiet and soft. The coffee cup warmed his hand as he walked along. He found himself near the ferry terminal, and ducked under the roof of the outdoor waiting area as the rain began to fall harder.

Islanders sat on benches chatting with each other. Very few tourists would be on the next couple of boats. These passengers were islanders ending their work day in Portland and returning to their homes out in the bay. Nick found himself envying them. They started and finished each working day with a trip across the water. He began to imagine how calming that would be, then realized that on any given day the ocean could be anything but calm. On some days it could batter the hell out of a ferry boat. That couldn't be a fun trip.

His mind drifted back to the afternoon. He tried to recall the events in order. He'd have to write them down when he got home. That always helped him. He thought of Isabel, alone and scared in that little shed. She didn't look like the type who would enjoy 'roughing it' either. She'd probably never been camping in her life.

He remembered how she had reacted when she heard Linda. That seemed strange. He could understand if Isabel had been annoyed with her sister-in-law, or even if she had ignored Linda altogether. Maybe Linda knew something that Isabel didn't want anyone to learn about? Did Linda see something happen at the house that night or even the next morning?

A ferry blasted its horn as it pulled away from the dock. Nick jumped at the sudden noise, jarred from his thoughts. He looked into his cup. Empty. His stomach growled. *'Stop thinking. Just go eat. Let all this stew a bit,'* he told himself. He smiled at the apt metaphor. With that, he stood, tossed his cup into a nearby trash can and headed home.

*Painting is just another way
of keeping a diary.*
~ Pablo Picasso

CHAPTER NINE

Kimberly wandered through the galleries of the Maine Museum of Art. She had hoped to see Dulcie, but was told that she was out for about an hour. Kimberly decided to wait. It was a good excuse to drift among the artwork.

She stopped at a meticulously painted trompe l'oeil. The painting showed a table with various objects strewn on it. At the center was a single rose. It looked so real that she found herself wanting to lift her hand and touch it.

"Looks like it just dropped there, doesn't it?"

Kimberly laughed, a lovely sound that echoed through the quiet room. She turned to face Dulcie.

"I had to force myself not to touch it. But I knew the guard over there," she nodded toward the corner, "would have yelled at me!"

"Anthony? He's a pussycat. He'd never yell. Right, Anthony?"

The man didn't turn his head but he did manage a half-smile. "I'd have yelled at her," he said.

"Well then, I'm glad I didn't provoke that!" Kimberly replied.

Dulcie smiled, but her expression quickly changed. "I'm glad you came by," she said more seriously, "Do you have a few minutes?"

"Absolutely. You have me intrigued!"

Dulcie led the way to her office. She closed the door behind them and gestured toward a chair. Kimberly sat down as Dulcie rounded her desk and sat down behind it. She leaned her arms on the desk and put her head down for a moment. "I knew this was a disaster before it even started!" Her voice was muffled. She looked up. "And now Logan's sister wants me to pay her for Logan's time. Well, for the time that he worked, not the entire time."

"What?" Kimberly exclaimed.

"I'll have to, of course. I just met with our lawyer. Logan did do part of the job, so we're obliged contractually, even if it's a payment to his estate. I'm just amazed that Linda would even think to ask. I mean, her brother just died. Doesn't she have more pressing matters to attend to?"

"She does, but someone like that works from a to-do list, even if it's a mental one," Kimberly replied. "Invoicing you is on the list, so she has to cross it off."

"Good point. She does carry that little notebook everywhere and she's constantly writing in it." Dulcie looked thoughtful for a moment. "Actually, I'd forgotten about the notebook. I'd love to have a look at it, if for no other reason than curiosity. I'd love to know why they're all here in the first place. Someone of Logan's stature doesn't just decide to grace us with his presence. They must have had a reason for coming here. Or Linda must have anyway, I don't think Logan and Isabel had much of a reason to do anything that they did, other than self-indulgence."

An odd look crossed Kimberly's face. Her eyebrows slid up and her eyes were wide.

"Kimberly, what are you thinking?" Dulcie asked. "You look like you're up to something!"

"Perhaps," she replied. "Dulcie, what if we visited Linda, just to check on her and make sure everything is going okay, and took a peek in the notebook? Or better yet, just borrowed it for a little while?"

"Kimberly! When I asked you to be my spy, I didn't think you'd consider anything like this!" Dulcie exclaimed. "But you do bring up an interesting idea, I must say!"

"Well, then! Here's the plan. We just stop by. Our excuse is to make sure she's all right. We'll ask if we can help with anything. One of us distracts her while the other nabs the notebook. Then we make a quick get-away before she notices!"

"And what if she does notice that one of us has it?" asked Dulcie.

"Good point." Kimberly was thoughtful for a moment. "I know! One of us can bring in a stack of folders or notebooks or something, and put it down near her notebook. Then we can say later that we scooped it up by accident."

"Hmmm! I like this! But we would need a reason to be carting in that stuff. Let me think," said Dulcie. She tapped her pen on the table for several seconds. "I've got it! I can bring the file with the Dumbarton's expenses and go over those things with her. I'll tell her that I need to review everything before getting a check to her. I'll also get her invoice then for Logan's work."

"Very good! Dulcie, it's a caper!" Kimberly said excitedly. "We're on a caper! Let's go now. Can you?"

Dulcie called out loudly, *"Rachel?"*

Several seconds later Rachel stuck her head in the door. "You rang?"

Dulcie laughed. "Yes. What am I doing for the next hour or so?"

Rachel disappeared, then reappeared. "A whole lotta nuthin."

Dulcie faked a dejected look. "I thought I was far more important than that!"

"Nope. Sorry," said Rachel.

"Let's remedy that situation. Kimberly and I are going on a little research trip. I'll be back inside of two hours. Can you hold all of my calls?"

"I'll try," said Rachel with a bemused look. She disappeared again.

"I'll drive so you can think," said Kimberly.

"Perfect," said Dulcie. She gathered several file folders and two spiral-bound notebooks that resembled Linda's. "Let's just hope that she has the notebook out somewhere that we can find easily." She stopped suddenly. "Kimberly, this is really wrong."

Kimberly nodded. "Yes it is, but everything about their coming here in the first place seems wrong. You said so yourself. Don't you feel as though you've been duped in some way?"

Dulcie looked thoughtful. "Yes, I do. All right. Let's go before I change my mind."

They were quiet during the short drive out to the cape. As Kimberly pulled into the driveway, Dulcie saw a curtain at the window twitch slightly. Linda was at home. They went to the back door and knocked. Linda opened it but did not immediately invite them in. "Can I help you with something?" she said sternly while standing in the doorway.

Dulcie smiled. "Hi Linda. Yes, I'm sorry to bother you. I probably should have called first. I need to review some receipts with you so that we can get you a reimbursement check. It's just a formality, but I'll need to have you sign off on them. Could we have a few minutes of your time?"

Linda did not move for a moment. "Of course," she finally said, stepping back inside. "Come in."

As they walked in Linda looked pointedly at Kimberly. "What brings you here?" she asked.

Kimberly thought quickly. "I asked Dulcie if I could come along to take pictures of the location I'd been painting. I didn't want to bother you, but since Dulcie was already coming…"

"Yes, yes. Whatever," Linda replied, now sounding annoyed. She waved her off.

Kimberly was glad that she had a camera on her phone. It would have been difficult to explain that she needed pictures, but hadn't brought a camera. She glanced quickly at Dulcie who nodded very slightly. As Kimberly walked from the back door to the front, she glanced around for Linda's notebook. She saw it on the kitchen counter. Kimberly quickly turned and saw that Linda's back was still toward her. She motioned to Dulcie and pointed at the notebook. The look in Dulcie's eye told her that she knew exactly what Kimberly was telling her. Kimberly continued along, letting herself out the front door.

"Can we just spread some of these things out on the kitchen counter? I can be quicker that way," said Dulcie.

Linda huffed her breath slightly but led the way into the kitchen. Dulcie quickly followed. She spotted Linda's notebook and set down her files next to it, positioning herself so that Linda was on the opposite side. She opened the first file folder, covering the notebook.

"All right, here's your rental agreement for the house, your grocery purchases, and the car rental. Just look this over, then sign here if they're correct." She pointed to the page while glancing out the window. Dulcie hoped that Kimberly would come back quickly. She couldn't delay for very long.

Linda scanned the sheet and signed. Dulcie put the next set of receipts out and again, Linda rapidly signed. *'One more set to go. Come on, Kimberly!'* she thought anxiously. Dulcie shuffled through the file trying to buy a bit more time. She brought out the final set of receipts just as Kimberly came back inside. As Linda signed, Dulcie looked at Kimberly and winked. Kimberly breezed by and went to the back door.

"Thanks so much, Linda. That's exactly what I needed," Kimberly said. "Also, Linda, I just wanted to express my condolences. We learned so much from Logan. He is… was an amazing talent. He'll be missed greatly."

Linda was caught off guard. She had not expected to hear praise for her brother, especially from one of the class members. She almost smiled as she turned toward Kimberly to thank her.

Dulcie saw her chance. With Linda's back turned she slid the notebook in between her files, picked up everything and moved toward the door. "Thanks Linda. I'll get these processed right away and get a check to you. So sorry to bother you!" She nearly tripped over Kimberly as they both pushed through the door. Linda's demeanor had changed back to her more typical, annoyed manner.

Kimberly slid in behind the wheel and started the car. Dulcie tried not to run around the car, walking as fast as she could to the passenger seat. She hadn't even closed the door before the car was moving.

When they reached the end of the street, Kimberly asked, "Do you have a camera on your phone?"

"Yes," Dulcie said. "Why?"

"Start taking pictures of the pages in that notebook. I have a feeling she might be right on our heels. She'll know it's gone within minutes, I'm guessing."

"Brilliant! I'm on it." She pulled out her camera and started snapping pictures, turning pages, then snapping more pictures. As she did, her phone rang. It was Linda.

Dulcie answered.

"You took my notebook," the angry voice sputtered.

"I'm sorry? What are you saying?" replied Dulcie, feigning innocence.

"When you left just now, you took my notebook with you. I'd like you to bring it back. Now."

"Oh my goodness! Hold on, let me just look through my things," she covered the phone for several seconds. Kimberly kept driving. "I'm so sorry, Linda! Yes, I have it right here. I must have scooped it up with my files. We're nearly back to the museum now. Would you like me to drive it back over to you, or do you want to come pick it up?"

"Bring it back," Linda barked and hung up.

Dulcie clicked off the phone and looked at Kimberly. "We have to turn around," she said.

"How much have you photographed?" Kimberly asked, still heading back to Portland.

"About half," Dulcie said.

Kimberly pulled into a parking lot and stopped the car. "Keep going. You snap, and I'll turn the pages." It took them about five minutes to finish. Kimberly started the car again.

"Wait! Let me just flip through these quickly to make sure they're clear!" Dulcie said as she went backwards through the images, swiping her finger across the phone rapidly. "Okay, I think we're good."

Kimberly pulled back onto the road and drove quickly to Linda's house. They weren't even in the driveway when Linda flew out of the door and hurried to the car. Dulcie lowered the window to hand the notebook to her. "I'm so glad you noticed right away so that we could..." she hadn't finished before Linda grabbed it and stormed back into the house without a word.

Before Kimberly had even pulled out of the driveway once again, both she and Dulcie burst out laughing.

☃

Willow had been reading when she heard a knock at the door. She sat bolt upright, silent. The knock came again. Silently, she tiptoed to the door and looked through the peephole. It was Bryce. *'How the hell does he know where I live?'* thought Willow.

"Hey, Willow? You home?" she heard him shout.

The last thing she wanted was trouble from her neighbors. They already disliked her. She yanked open the door. "What do you want?" she asked warily.

"Thought you might want to get a beer," he said.

"You couldn't call me for that?"

"Didn't have your number."

"But you know where I live?" she was becoming annoyed.

"Yeah, I saw it on a list for the master class. It wasn't public, don't worry. I'm just nosy."

Willow eyed him with some disdain, but then her look softened. "Hang on, I need to get my bag," she said. She closed the door and scooted into the bathroom. She ran her hand through her hair so that it spiked up a bit more. Then she grabbed a denim jacket and her bag and opened the door again.

"Where are we going?" she said, locking the door behind her.

"Wherever you want," he said.

"The Dock?"

"Sure." They walked down the stairs and out the front door in silence.

"So, pretty insane way to end a class, you think?" Bryce said.

"You have no idea," Willow replied. Bryce wrinkled his brow. "You probably don't know the latest. About Isabel," she added. Willow suddenly remembered how Bryce had admired Isabel and even seemed to flirt with her at one point. Willow was annoyed with herself that she brought it up.

"She's a piece of work," he said with some disdain.

Willow was surprised by his reaction. They turned into the bar. It was nearly empty. They sat on high wooden stools that had been battered from years of use. Willow plopped her bag on the empty stool next to her.

A large pot-bellied man with a scruff of new growth on his chin that he had obviously missed while shaving shuffled over. "What can I get ya?" he said wiping the counter in front of them.

"Couple of beers," said Bryce. He pointed to one of the taps.

The bartender looked at Willow. "Got any ID, kid?"

She narrowed her eyes and let out an exasperated sigh before she reached into her bag. Locating her wallet she pulled it out and flashed him her driver's license. He looked at it for longer than necessary, then eyed her closely over the top of it. "You sure this is you," he said. "You don't look like a *Willow*."

She opened her mouth to tell him exactly what he looked like, but Bryce interjected, "Lots of types of Willow. She isn't the weeping kind, trust me!"

The bartender laughed and gave her back her license. He pulled on the tap and filled two pint glasses.

Willow took a long drink. She didn't realize how thirsty she was. The beer felt very cold as it quickly made its way into her empty stomach. It gave her confidence. "So what do you really think of our friend Isabel?" she asked.

Bryce licked the foam from his top lip. "Honestly? She knows how to get what she wants, but I got the feeling that she's in over her head on this one. Not sure why I think that."

Willow nodded. "Me too. So you don't know what happened with her after Logan got carted off?"

Bryce shook his head.

"She ran off and hid, in an abandoned shack," Willow replied.

Bryce put down his bear. "That's weird. How come?"

"Don't know," said Willow. "But she called me and said she was scared. Then the cops talked to me and wanted me to get more out of her. I backed off. No way was I gonna get involved." She took another sip of her beer.

"So did they find her?"

Willow nodded as she swallowed. "The cops had me call her with that museum lady there, then I handed off the phone to her. Isabel told her where she was. It was in some shed up the beach form their house. Everyone raced down there. Now she's at the museum lady's house, I think." Willow took another drink of beer.

Bryce looked thoughtful. "Huh. Why did she hide, I wonder?"

Willow slapped her hand down on the bar, making Bryce jump. The bartender eyed her. She glared back at him. "I totally forgot that part!" she exclaimed as she turned back to Bryce. "She thought she'd killed Logan. She put turpentine in his drink. I guess she just wanted to make him sick so he'd stop drinking, but she thought it killed him. That's why she ran off."

Bryce was very interested now. "So did it?" he asked.

Willow shook her head. "Don't know. Don't care."

Bryce inwardly groaned. He was getting nowhere. "And she hasn't talked to you since?"

"Nope. I told the cops I wanted out. It was this big guy. Johnson, I think his name was. I actually thought he was okay, but I still didn't want to talk with any of them again. Haven't heard anything from them since, so that's fine by me."

Bryce decided to change the subject. They talked about painting as they finished their beer, then he walked Willow home. He asked if she wanted to have dinner with him later in the week and was mildly surprised to see her looking shy. But she agreed. He left it at that.

Bryce walked aimlessly through the city. He was in a difficult position. He knew something, yet he wasn't sure if it was really important. The last thing he wanted to do was talk to the police, though. He'd had a run-in with them once before, a speeding situation that had involved a bit of a chase during his days as a joy-riding youth. He had skipped out on the final weekend of community service that they'd given him instead of jail time. He really didn't want them to dredge that up again.

What he knew was nagging at him, though. Johnson. Willow had said that's who she had talked to, and that he had seemed okay. If he had put Willow at ease, maybe he would be the guy to talk to? He shook his head. No, he had to think it over more.

೦෪

Nick had read the autopsy report three times. Logan Dumbarton had died from heart failure. Yet he did not seem to have any kind of heart condition. It could happen, but something told Nick that it was all wrong. He needed some answers.

Nick looked up the number of the coroner who had signed off on Logan's autopsy. He dialed, hoping that he wouldn't get voicemail.

"Dr. Kraus!" a brisk voice said.

"Hello, doctor. I'm Nicholas Black, detective with the Portland Police. Could I ask a few questions about Logan Dumbarton?"

"Sure. You have about seven minutes. Maybe eight. I have to pick up my daughter from ballet class."

Nick stifled a snorting sound. Somehow he couldn't imagine a coroner at a ballet school. Or even having a daughter, for that matter.

Quickly collecting his thoughts, Nick said, "Dumbarton's death was determined as heart failure, but he didn't have a known heart condition. That seems odd."

"Yup. But it happens."

"He was a heavy drinker. Would that have affected his heart at all?"

"Sure. You're talking about alcoholic cardiomyopathy. The weird thing is that he really didn't show signs of it. My guess would be that he only started the drinking recently."

"That's interesting. Overall, did anything strike you as odd? He'd ingested turpentine, I know. Did that seem to affect him?"

"Nope. It might have made him sick to his stomach if he'd lived long enough. Oh, but there's one thing that you might not have picked up on. It's in the report but not obvious to the layman. He suffered from hypogonadism."

"That sounds like enlarged…"

The doctor chuckled. "It isn't what you're thinking. Basically, it boils down to low testosterone. He was recently married, right?"

"Yes," said Nick, slowly.

"My bet is that the marriage probably hasn't been consummated."

"Huh!" It was the only response Nick could come up with.

"Anything else?" the doctor asked.

Nick was still at a loss for words. "No, nothing else. Thanks, doctor."

"Anytime," he responded.

Nick put down his phone on the desk in front of him, then picked it up again immediately. He tapped on it, and it began ringing. His partner answered.

"Hey, where are you?" asked Nick.

"Havin' a decent cup of coffee," Johnson replied.

"Good. Stay there. I'll be right down."

Nick left the police station and jogged down the street. He pushed open the door of the coffee shop and immediately spotted Johnson at their usual booth. Johnson looked up from the cinnamon danish he'd just ordered. "Got somethin'?"

Nick sat down. "I don't really know. You tell me." He related what the coroner had said.

Johnson put down his fork. He leaned back in the seat. The vinyl cushion squeaked beneath him as it rubbed against the wooden bench. "So you're saying that the heart attack was totally '*normal*' if you can call it that."

"Right."

"But the big news is that most likely the marriage was in name only."

"Yes."

Johnson folded his arms, resting them on his large stomach. "Well that puts a spin on things for sure, now, doesn't it."

"It does. The question is, what kind of spin? Something tells me that in spite of what the coroner said, that heart attack wasn't *natural*."

"Can anything bring on a heart attack without leaving any trace?" asked Johnson.

"Good question. Probably. I don't know for sure, but I'll find out," said Nick.

Johnson leaned forward again, the lure of the danish too much to ignore any longer. He took a big bite and washed it down with a large swig of coffee. "Go get

145

one," he said, hoisting his cup in front of Nick as an example, "And let's think about this."

Nick decided on an espresso. It was in a tiny cup, but it gave him the jolt he desperately needed. He returned to the table, balancing the diminutive cup on the saucer. Johnson looked at it and rolled his eyes.

"Doubt you'd be man enough to drink this," said Nick in response.

"Won't even go there," Johnson replied. "So, that young lady, Isabel, we need to talk to her next, right?"

"Right," said Nick. "I don't totally buy that story that she was hiding because she thought she killed her husband. Something else scared her, and it wasn't a dead man. She did not want to talk to her sister-in-law, that's for sure."

"Was she scared of her do you think?" asked Johnson.

"I can't see why. Could be. Heck, I'd be scared of her. But she'd been living there with her so I don't know why she would suddenly be scared." Nick finished his espresso in one mouthful and made a face as he swallowed it. "Bitter," he said. "But it makes me think better."

"Rots your stomach, too," added Johnson.

Nick ignored him. "I'm probably wasting our time here. Most likely he dropped from a heart attack, end of story. I should just let this one go."

"Ya can't though, can you," said Johnson.

Nick closed his eyes and sighed. "No," he said. "No, I can't." He opened his eyes and looked intently into the empty cup. "So let's say someone gave him something during the day, or the evening, that eventually induced the heart attack. That leaves only Linda or Isabel."

"Unless he took something himself. Maybe he had some drugs someone gave him?"

"Good point. I'll find out if he had any regular doctors in London, and if anything was prescribed. There'll be nothing, of course, but we have to rule it out."

"How are we going to find out who his doctor was?" asked Johnson.

"That's the sticky part. I suppose we'll have to ask Linda."

"Let me do that," said Johnson with a faint smile. "I'd love to take her on. Sounds like she needs to come down a peg."

"Go easy," said Nick. "She just lost her brother."

"Yeah, okay. But she could have been the one who did him in, ya know."

"True, but I don't think so. His will was changed so that everything went to Isabel. Linda gained far more by managing his career while he was alive," said Nick.

"All right. I'll work the Linda angle and find out about doctors. You go talk to Isabel," said Johnson stuffing the last bite of danish into his mouth. "Oh, and *don't* go too easy on her! You can be way too soft sometimes."

"My methods always work in the end, and you know it," Nick said, trying to hide a smile. "I'll give you a call later."

"Can't wait," Johnson replied without gusto.

The moment Nick left, Johnson's phone rang. He didn't like to talk on it in the coffee shop. He grabbed it and quickly made his way to the door. "Johnson!" he barked into it.

He heard someone inhale, as if caught off guard. "This is Detective Johnson?" said a man's voice.

"I just said that," Johnson replied.

"Okay. I'm Bryce Bartlett. I was in that art class with Logan Dumbarton. I'd like to talk to you about something."

Johnson's demeanor changed instantly. He stood up straight and focused intently on the sidewalk in front of him. "Sure, I can meet you right now. Where are you?" he said.

"I'm over at the Dock. The bar on Commercial Street. You know it?" said Bryce.

"Yup. Sit tight – I'll be right there."

Bryce put his phone back in his pocket. His wandering had led him right back to the bar where he was having another beer. He'd nearly finished it before he worked up the nerve to call.

Johnson barreled down toward the water and made it to the bar faster than anyone who saw his size would have expected. He strode through the door and blinked in the comparative darkness.

Bryce considered pretending that he was someone else for a moment. Johnson had spied him, though, and somehow knew who he was. "Dammit," thought Bryce. "He's probably looked me up in some police database already."

Johnson hoisted himself onto the barstool. "Mr. Bartlett?" he asked.

"Yeah," said Bryce.

The bartender came over. "Get him another on me," said Johnson. "And I'll have a ginger ale."

"You don't drink?" asked Bryce.

"I'm on duty," said Johnson. "So, you wanted to tell me something?"

"Yeah, it's probably not important, though. Shouldn't have wasted your time."

"I'll be the judge of that," said Johnson jovially. "Lemme have it."

Bryce took a sip of the beer that had just been put in front of him. "Well, it's kind of weird. When I came to the first plein air painting session, for that class with Logan Dumbarton, I could have sworn I'd seen his sister before. Linda Dumbarton. It was driving me nuts because I couldn't place her. Then I remembered, finally. It was a couple of months ago. I work at a gallery up on Congress Street. She came in with what looked like a Logan Dumbarton painting. She wanted to sell it. The gallery owner said that it looked like one of Dumbarton's and the signature was right, but the lady didn't have any authentication for it. She was pretty mad when she found out we couldn't sell. The owner said she could sell it as a possible Dumbarton, or as a potential student of Dumbarton's work. Those would go for about a quarter of the amount a Dumbarton would bring in, though, if that. The lady left in a huff with the painting, and I didn't think about it again.

"When I remembered, I asked Logan about it during one of his critiques. He just gave me this arrogant look and said I didn't know what I was talking about. He said his sister hadn't been to the states for two years. Then he proceeded to rip apart my painting technique in about twenty different ways. He could be pretty brutal. Didn't bother me, though. I knew he was an ass."

Johnson swirled his ginger ale glass around on the bar. "How certain are you that it was her?" he asked.

"Pretty darned sure," Bryce said.

Johnson was thoughtful. "Thanks for getting in touch," he said, throwing a few dollar bills on the table. "I'll call you if I need anything else." He slid off the bar stool and lumbered out.

Bryce breathed a sigh of relief. Maybe they hadn't checked up on him after all.

CB

Nick sat on the couch in Dulcie's townhouse beside Isabel. Dulcie came in with two mugs of tea. She gently put the mugs down on the table in front of them. Then she disappeared into the kitchen, and reappeared with her own mug.

When Dulcie sat down, Nick turned to Isabel. "Tell us everything," he said simply.

Isabel took a deep breath. Her dark hair gleamed as a ray of sunlight came through the window and radiated among the ebony strands. She took a sip of tea and looked back and forth between them. "All right. Here's everything," she said. "I met Linda when they were in India. I was there on a photo shoot, and Logan had a show there. We met at a party. Linda was so nice to me. I found out that they lived in London, quite near me. When we were back in England, Linda got in touch with me again. She and I got together several times and, well, a relationship started. I'm a lesbian, you see, and so is Linda."

Nick and Dulcie exchanged surprised glances.

Isabel continued. "Linda came up with the plan that I should entice Logan and get him to marry me. Then she and I could be together, plus I wouldn't have to worry about money any more. Logan seemed nice enough, so I thought it would all be fine.

"The biggest problem was that I wasn't attracted to Logan, for obvious reasons. Linda said not to worry. She said that he wasn't able to perform, that he never could. I wondered why we had to keep our relationship secret from Logan, but Linda told me it was because he was very old-fashioned and would disapprove entirely.

"Linda arranged for Logan to go to a specific party in London, and I was supposed to attract him, but be aloof at the same time. She said that he had already remarked about me after he saw me in some of the advertising campaigns that I had modeled for. Whatever I did must have worked. He started calling me and I dated him, then I married him.

"Everything seemed fine at first, but then Logan started drinking. He was horrible when he drank. It was like he became a different person. And once he started, he just couldn't stop. He ordered everyone around and was so rude. I didn't know what to do.

"Linda suggested that we get away from London for a change of scene. She said that it might help Logan to stop the drinking. But it didn't. I even tried to take his work in a different direction by planting suggestions of abstract nudes and the ocean and so forth. It worked for a little while. He seemed focused on that, especially with me posing. But it didn't last.

"I finally couldn't stand it any longer. I knew that I had to do something drastic. I put turpentine in his drink that night before he died. I thought that if it made him really nauseated, he wouldn't be able to so much as look at a gin and tonic again.

"And fortunately, that wasn't what killed him," said Dulcie. "Look Isabel, I think anyone could sympathize with you, especially after what he did to you. I don't know what you may have said or done to provoke it, but no man should hit his wife the way he did. I felt so horrible for you when I saw that bruise."

Now Isabel looked confused. She opened her mouth, then closed it again.

"Isabel, what is it?" asked Dulcie.

Isabel looked down into her tea. "Logan didn't hit me," she said quietly. "Linda did."

Dulcie suddenly remember the loud slap that she had heard when Linda was trying to wake Logan on that terrible morning. She thought about how she herself would attempt to revive someone. She might try slapping them, but she knew that even if she thought they had passed out, or worse, she could never have possibly hit them so hard. Linda had delivered the blow easily. As though she had done it before.

Now it made sense. "Isabel, is that why you ran away? Was Linda hurting you?"

Huge tears began to run down Isabel's cheeks. She gulped back a sob. "She had done it a few times, when she got angry. She was always so apologetic and remorseful afterward. But that was another reason why I convinced Logan that I should pose nude for him. If I did, any bruise would be there, plain to see. It kept Linda from hitting me."

"Why didn't you just tell Logan?"

"He would have been disgusted by my relationship with Linda. Don't you realize? We duped him, played him for a fool! He would have thrown me out. He had to keep Linda because she ran his life, but I would have been tossed out like garbage and worse off than when I started. Linda made it clear that she could easily spread some pretty awful rumors around about me and destroy my reputation in the industry. My contracts have been diminishing as I've become older. It seems that everyone wants to photograph youth. I've needed every job I could get, until I married Logan."

Nick and Dulcie were silent for a moment. Then, they both spoke at once. "Sorry," said Nick. "Go ahead."

"Isabel, Linda told me that the plan was originally for Logan to come here on his own. But you're saying that you all intended to come together from the beginning."

"Yes, we did," said Isabel. She sniffed loudly. "Maybe you misunderstood her?"

"Maybe," Dulcie murmured.

"Isabel, you are aware that Logan changed his will?" Nick asked. "You inherit everything. That is motive to kill him, although you've been cleared of that by the autopsy."

"I didn't know about the will until he died. Honestly!" she protested.

"Linda only benefitted from him while he was alive," Nick continued.

"I know, and it looks quite bad for me, but really this has to be just an unfortunate accident! I only put the turpentine in his drink. Really!"

Dulcie leaned forward. "When did he start drinking?" she asked.

"It was a couple of weeks after we were married. I remember he didn't even have champagne at our wedding, although it was quite a quick, small affair. Still, I thought that was strange since someone brought a bottle and I certainly had a glass," Isabel said.

Nick made a show of finishing his tea, putting down his mug, and looking at his watch. "Thanks so much for your time, both of you," he said. He stood and looked down at Isabel. "I don't think you have anything to worry about," he said. "Thanks for the tea, Dulcie." He widened his eyes at her as he turned away. She quickly grabbed his mug along with her own and followed him out.

Nick said nothing but gestured toward his phone. She got the message and nodded. "Thanks again," Nick then said out loud and left.

Dulcie returned to the living room. "Isabel, you look exhausted. Would you like to lie down for a while? I need to run to the grocery store, so it will be nice and quiet while I'm gone."

Isabel smiled. "It's always nice and quiet here. I really appreciate everything you've done for me. Will you wake me when you come back?"

"Of course," Dulcie said. She picked up her purse and her keys. "Lock the door if you like. I have my key." She opened the door and stepped onto the porch. She heard the door close and the lock click behind her.

Dulcie forced herself to walk slowly down the street. When she reached the corner she dug into her purse and pulled out her phone. Quickly, she called Nick.

"So, what do you think?" he said without any formality of a greeting. "That was quite a revelation."

"You could say that!" Dulcie replied. "There seems to be a whole lot of *'back-story'* here. Still, Logan's death is pretty clean-cut, isn't it? I mean, he died of a heart attack. What else is there to know?"

It was a good question, and Nick didn't have a good answer. "Something just feels wrong," he finally answered.

Dulcie was frustrated, and it aggravated her. "Nick, you can't just drag this along because of a feeling," she said. "At some point you need to just drop the whole thing and let people get on with their lives."

She was right. He knew it. And he knew the hidden message behind what she said, even if she hadn't intended it. She wanted to get on with her life, without him. He had lost any chance with her.

"Yes. I will. I'm going to close this case first thing tomorrow morning. They can take Logan's body back to London or wherever they want to bury him." He felt as though he had been beaten.

"I think it's a good decision," Dulcie said in a kinder voice.

"Yes. You're right. Thanks again, Dulcie. Bye." She heard the phone click off.

Dulcie felt terrible, but what could she do? She looked back at her phone, then remembered the photos she had taken of Linda's notebook. It had been a silly idea to do that. She smiled remembering Kimberly's description of it: a caper. Dulcie walked slowly along the street, swiping through the images of Linda's notebook. She could barely see them on the tiny screen. It didn't matter. It seemed to be ordinary, day-to-day reminders and to-do lists, the stuff of everyday life, important to no one but the person writing it all down. She put the phone in her pocket.

Dulcie didn't really need to go to the grocery store. It was a beautiful day, sunny and warm. She had called in to Rachel and taken the day off. Dulcie tried to convince herself it was to make herself available for Isabel, but if she was honest, she simply needed time to think.

She walked along the brick sidewalk, letting her thoughts drift. The events of the week had all been so strange. In spite of the sunshine, the gentle ocean breeze, the clouds flitting through an otherwise clear blue sky, Dulcie felt permeated with dread. Once she acknowledged this, anger crept in. Why had they invaded her life? Why had they brought their horrible problems and hatred into her world?

The worst of it, however, was him. Nick. The one person that she did not want to see again. The one person that she had been trying to push out of her mind. The one person that had broken her trust.

It was stupid. She had told herself this hundreds of times already. Originally, she had developed a small crush on Nicholas Black, and he might have reciprocated some feelings, but nothing happened. He had not betrayed her. Logically, she kept reminding herself of this. Her heart felt differently.

Dulcie realized that she was hungry. She saw a coffee shop ahead and decided a bit of indulgence in the form of some decadent pastry was what she needed to pull her out of this funk. She went in and stood at the counter, staring into the glass case for several moments.

"I'd take the éclair," a low voice said from behind her. She whirled around. It was Nick. *'Why, dammit?'* she thought. Her face must have registered her despair, because he put up both hands and said, "Whoa! Just a suggestion!"

Dulcie sighed, but said nothing.

Nick stepped up to the cashier. "Could I have two éclairs and two coffees please?"

"What makes you think that's what I wanted?" Dulcie finally stammered.

"What makes you think I ordered for you?" Nick replied.

Dulcie softened. "All right. I'm sorry. I'm on edge these days."

"Tell me about it," said Nick. He handed both plates to Dulcie and picked up both cups. "Want to sit over there?" he gestured toward a table at the window.

Dulcie smiled in spite of herself. "You never sit at a table," she said.

"Correction. Johnson never sits at a table. And I'm usually with him. Not exactly the most attractive date."

Nick blushed, realizing he'd just suggested that they were on a date. "I mean…"

"I know what you mean."

The sat on the metal chairs and Dulcie bit into her éclair. "I haven't had one of these in ages. I love them, but I never get them."

"Why?" Nick asked.

Dulcie shook her head. "Too many calories. I'm constantly restraining myself. I'd be the size of this table if I don't pay attention."

"I can't imagine that. Besides, you have nothing to worry about," Nick said. He blushed again, cleared his throat, and changed the subject. "I've been talking to Johnson about this whole case. He thinks I should close it, too. I keep having this nagging feeling that I'm missing something, but he says that sometimes, they really are open and shut."

"I have to say I'm inclined to agree with him," Dulcie said. "I know what you're feeling, though. Earlier, I could have sworn that Linda was up to something. Kimberly and I even hatched a plan to steal the notebook that she's always writing in. We actually pulled it off. Kimberly called it a *caper*." Dulcie laughed.

"Do I want to hear this? I'm not sure you should be telling me that you stole something."

"It's okay," Dulcie said. "We brought it right back, literally within minutes. Of course, I took pictures of all of the pages first."

Nick had just taken a drink of coffee and was about to put down the cup. His hand froze in midair. He swallowed hard. "Say that again?"

Dulcie glanced at him curiously. "We knew that Linda would notice that the notebook was missing right away, and she did. While Kimberly was driving, I kept flipping through the pages and taking pictures.

Linda called me while we were still in the car, so we turned right around and brought it back." Dulcie reached into her pocket and pulled out her phone. She brought up the images of the notebook on the screen. "But I managed to photograph every page. They're right here," she said.

Nick realized that his coffee cup was still hovering above the table. He put it down gently. His mind was racing. He tried to make it stop. Logan Dumbarton's death was an open and shut case. True, it had some odd angles, but the death itself was simple. Why then, couldn't he let it go?

"Dulcie, I know this is asking a lot, but could you look through all of those images and read what she wrote?"

Dulcie was confused. "Why? I'd be happy to, but why would you want that at this point? I thought the case was closed?"

"It is, nearly. I just want to put every last doubt to rest. And this is one last doubt."

"All right, I'll look through things tonight. I'm not sure what I'm looking for, but I'll look, nonetheless," Dulcie said.

"Just look for things that strike you as anomalies. You knew these three people better than anyone else here, even if it was for a short time. See if something jumps out at you."

"Yes, I'll do it. But if nothing does, will the case still be closed? Can we move on?"

There it was again. The words: *move on.*

'*Fine,*' Nick thought. *'Message received.*' "Yes," he said aloud. "We can move on."

Dulcie nodded but he noticed she did not smile. She finished her éclair, quietly thanked him, and left.

CB

At seven o'clock that evening, Dulcie sat at her computer while eating chicken fried rice straight from the carton. Isabel had already retreated to the guest room with tea, toast, and a book. Dulcie had ordered several extra items with her Chinese delivery even after Isabel had demurred, but she still wanted nothing more than her tea and toast. Dulcie eyed the half-eaten carton, thinking *'that's why she's about fifteen pounds lighter.'* Then she shrugged her shoulders and reached for an egg roll.

She had downloaded the images from her phone to her laptop. Now she read through them, one after another. Nothing seemed to be unusual, although she had not reached anything that concerned their trip to Portland.

Dulcie had just taken a large bite of egg roll when she heard a knock on the door. *'Who on earth...?'* she thought. She peeked through the crack in the curtain. Linda stood there. When she saw Dulcie look outside, she stooped down and glared back at her. *'Guess I can't pretend I'm not home,'* Dulcie thought with annoyance. She opened the door.

"Yes, Linda? I'm surprised to see you at this hour," Dulcie said. Suddenly she remembered that her laptop was still open. She hoped that Linda couldn't see it from where she was.

"I need to talk to Isabel. She isn't answering her phone," Linda announced.

"She's gone to bed already. I'd rather not disturb her. I'll speak to her in the morning and let her know you were here," Dulcie said, standing firmly in the doorway.

"I need to talk to her now. It's important," Linda protested.

Linda's manner angered her. She certainly was pushy. Then Dulcie remembered what Isabel had said about Linda hitting her. Dulcie stretched her petite frame as tall as she could. "I will not disturb her now. If you would like me to give her a message, I can certainly make sure that she receives it."

Linda's eyes bulged angrily. "Tell her to call me," she blurted out.

Dulcie shook her head. "Nope. Sorry, but it will have to be more specific than that."

Now Linda looked furious. Her face grew red. For a brief moment, Dulcie wondered if Linda would hit her the way she had Isabel.

At last she managed to say, "It concerns the body of my brother who, if you will recall, recently died. I would think that you could show a bit more consideration given that fact. The coroner is releasing him, and I would like to have him cremated. I've scheduled it for the day after tomorrow. As his wife, I need Isabel to sign off on the transfer."

Dulcie was surprised. She did not have experience with the matter, but she had always assumed that if nothing was written in a will, it was the spouse's decision as to what happened to the body. At the moment, however, she thought it best not to challenge Linda. "I'll give Isabel the message," she said. "Have a good evening." Dulcie closed the door firmly and pulled the curtain tightly across. She didn't move until she heard Linda walking down the front steps.

"Is she gone?" Dulcie heard the voice from the darkness at the top of the stairs.

"Yes, Isabel. She's gone."

"Thanks for not letting her in." Isabel wrapped her robe tightly around her and sat down on the top step. "I don't think I ever want to see her again."

"I wouldn't blame you," Dulcie replied. "Did you hear what she said?"

"Yes, and I must say that I'm confused. I thought that it was the spouse who made the determination. I don't think Logan would have wanted to be cremated."

"Do you think Linda is doing it simply to expedite everything or, and I don't mean to sound crass, to save money?" Dulcie asked.

Isabel's laugh was hollow. "That's something she would do. But, she probably just wants to move everything along. That's what she does best." Isabel sighed. "I don't know how I got caught up in this mess. I don't know what I saw in her. She seemed so nice at first, and she just took care of everything. She took care of me."

"You're not the first to be caught in a bad relationship. And you won't be the last, unfortunately," Dulcie said.

Isabel nodded almost imperceptibly. "Yes. I do believe you're correct." She stood with some difficulty, as though she was too exhausted to hold her own weight. "Goodnight, Dulcie. And thanks again."

"Of course. Sleep well," Dulcie replied.

She watched Isabel disappear back into the darkness, then returned to her desk. She dug into the fried rice again and flipped to the next page of Linda's notebook. The date was about three months before the Dumbarton's arrival in Maine. Dulcie read through the notes, then saw: *BOS 14:10 arr, PWM 17:05.*

She knew those codes. They were the airport codes for Boston and Portland. Why did Linda have these codes written down, as though she had scheduled flights before she had even spoken to Dulcie? She jotted down the information on her notepad and continued on. Three days later, Linda had written, *Portside Gallery, Congress Street* along with a telephone number. "That looks odd, too," Dulcie murmured. She wrote it down.

The next several pages contained nothing although Dulcie learned that Linda suffered from nocturnal leg cramps and took some sort of medication for them. There were notes of her conversations with Dulcie, and airline reservations for all three of them. *'That's odd as well,'* thought Dulcie. *'I know she told me that she had expected Logan to be going alone. Clearly she lied about that.'*

Dulcie found nothing else that seemed strange while reading through the rest of the pages. The only other item that she noted was a company name in Portland that she'd never heard of. It looked like a warehouse or storage facility.

Yawning, Dulcie picked up her Chinese dinner containers and brought them to the kitchen. She filled the electric kettle and flipped on its switch. Tea would be very nice before bed. While she waited for the water to boil, she thought of calling Nick. *'He said he would close the case tomorrow. I should at least report in,'* she thought. She went back to her desk and checked the time. Nine o'clock. Not too late. She dialed his number.

"Hey, Dulcie," he answered quietly.

'Dammit,' thought Dulcie. *'Why does he have such a nice voice?'* Aloud she said, "I just wanted to let you know what I found in Linda's notebook. Not much really. She wrote down The Boston and Portland airport codes, and times next to each. That was about three

months ago. No flight numbers, but it looks like she was looking into flights?"

"Now that's interesting," Nick interrupted.

"Why?" Dulcie asked.

"Because Bryce Bartlett thought he saw her about three months ago in the gallery where he works."

"Would that be Portside Gallery, on Congress?"

"Is that written down too?" Now Nick was very interested.

"As a matter of fact, it is," Dulcie said. "I only noticed a couple of other things. First, it looks as though all three intended to come here from the start. Linda told me that she and Isabel only came at the last minute on Logan's insistence. That's why my assistant, Rachel, had to scramble at the last minute to find them a bigger house."

"That is strange, but it may not mean anything. What was the other thing?"

"Nothing really. It looks like the name of some warehouse or storage facility? Holden's Holdings."

"Yup, I know it. It's a self-storage place."

"She just has the name and phone number written down."

"Okay. Anything else?" Nick asked.

"Not in her notebook, but she actually showed up on my doorstep earlier this evening. She wanted to see Isabel."

"Did she? See her, I mean?"

"Absolutely not. Isabel had gone to bed early and I wasn't about to disturb her. I made Linda tell me exactly what she wanted. It seems that the coroner is releasing Logan's body, and she wants to have him cremated. Right away. She was quite upset because she can't have it done without Isabel's consent. I think Linda has handled everything for so long, she can't face the fact that someone else might have some authority," Dulcie concluded.

"I think you're right. Have you told Isabel?"

"Yes, she heard Linda but stayed upstairs. She doesn't like the idea of a cremation. She didn't think that Logan would have wanted it."

"Her opinion is the only one that matters," Nick said. "So that's it? Anything else?"

"I'm sorry to say that I have nothing else." Dulcie heard Nick sigh.

"All right. I guess that's that. I'll wrap everything up in the morning. Thanks again, Dulcie."

"No problem. Goodnight, Nick." She said.

The teakettle was boiling rapidly. Dulcie went into the kitchen and went through the ritual of making tea. It involved selecting which kind, deciding which mug she would use, putting in the teabag, pouring the water slowly… the process always calmed her.

Linda's sudden appearance that evening had made her nervous. Why hadn't she simply called? If Isabel wouldn't answer her phone, why hadn't Linda called Dulcie? And why did she want to have Logan cremated, regardless of Isabel's wishes? Maybe the thought of travelling back to London with her brother's body was difficult for her. Still…

Dulcie sipped her tea and looked back through the pages of Linda's notebook. Nothing else seemed to jump out at her. She yawned. The page that mentioned the leg cramps was open in front of her. Dulcie had leg cramps from time to time. Once she even woke up in the middle of the night with one. She wondered what someone would take for them.

She switched to the Internet search page on her computer and typed in *leg cramp medication*. A few muscle relaxants were listed. Then she came across a reference to quinine. *'That's strange,'* thought Dulcie. *'I always thought that was what they gave people in the old days for malaria.'* It indicated that in the US, the medication was no longer allowed to be prescribed for cramps, but was still available in the UK. *'I wonder if that's what she took,'* thought Dulcie.

Quinine. Dulcie knew it was a very old remedy. She remembered Cassandra, the woman that she had spoken with in Bermuda. They had talked about the teas and potions of the old days. *'Yet we use the same things even today,'* thought Dulcie.

Quinine. It was used to flavor tonic water. Gin and tonic. Dulcie put down her tea and leaned forward. She typed in *'quinine side effects.'* A list of various side effects appeared. There seemed to be many, everything from anxiety and behavior change to slurred speech similar to drunkenness. One more caught Dulcie's eye: rapid or irregular heartbeat.

Cassandra's words now came back to her. "They call it *Young Man's Death.*" She hadn't been talking about quinine, though. Why would Dulcie remember those words in particular? She sat back in her chair again. Something was stirring in the back of her mind. What if… ?

Dulcie grabbed her phone. She hoped that Nick was still awake.

"Something else?" he said without any greeting.

"Nick! Yes, possibly. Linda had noted something about a leg cramp medication. I don't know what it was, but I just looked up possibilities. One that they still prescribe in the UK is quinine. It's the same thing as in tonic water. One of the possible side effects can have an effect on the heart. What if someone put extra quinine in his drink? It's bitter, but he may not have noticed if he'd already had a few. Or maybe they spaced it out over a few drinks? Could that have killed him?"

"Interesting. Hang on, let me check the autopsy report again."

Dulcie heard papers rustling.

"This lists his stomach contents, and gin and tonic are there, but no mention of quinine."

"Would they have looked for it specifically if they already knew he'd had tonic water?" Dulcie asked.

"Good question. I don't know."

"The other question is, who would have put it in his drink? It could have been Linda or Isabel." Dulcie felt a chill run down her spine. Had Isabel killed her husband after all? Was the turpentine a front to throw them off course? Were she and Linda working together? Did Linda poison him herself? Or did he actually die of a heart attack?

Nick was thinking the same things. "Dulcie, Isabel is still there, right?"

"Yes," Dulcie said hesitantly.

"Does she know that you have Linda's notebook?" Nick asked.

"I don't think so," Dulcie said. She had left her laptop open earlier, however. And Isabel could have overheard her talking with Nick.

"But you're not sure," Nick said.

"No, I'm not sure." Dulcie realized that she had begun shaking.

"Dulcie, I want you to lock your bedroom door tonight. If you can't lock it, barricade it with something. I'm also going to post someone outside your house. If you have any trouble, just scream as loud as you can and they'll come running."

"Do you really think…?"

"I don't know what to think. But I just want you to be safe."

"Okay," she whispered. "But now I'm scared."

"Just do everything you'd normally do. Chances are very good that I'm totally wrong here. Keep the phone by the bed and call any time, even in the middle of the night. Don't hesitate."

"I won't. Hesitate, that is. Thanks, Nick."

"Sure thing. You'll be fine. Just be careful. Okay? Goodnight, Dulcie"

"Night," Dulcie answered feebly. She quickly got up and got herself ready for bed. She brought her laptop and phone with her. Once inside her bedroom, she locked the door and dragged the heavy wooden bureau as far as she could in front of it. She turned out the light. Before she got into bed, she looked out the window. A police car had pulled up across the street. That made her feel better.

Tommy sat in the cruiser, staring at the townhouse on the opposite side of the street. He didn't take his eyes off it. His partner in the seat next to him was snoring softly, an empty coffee cup in his hand. Tommy hadn't had any coffee. The excitement of being sent on this "mission" as Detective Black had called it, was all that he needed to keep him awake for the rest of the night.

To send light into
the darkness of men's hearts
- such is the duty of the artist.
~ Robert Schumann

CHAPTER TEN

Dulcie slept very little. During the night she remembered Isabel's terrible black eye. *'She would never be in league with Linda if she had been hit like that,'* Dulcie thought. Comforted by this, she fell asleep, only to wake again an hour later immediately realizing that Logan could have given her the black and she had simply lied about it. The entire night went on in much the same manner. Every creak and noise in the house made her strain her ears, wondering if someone would try to open the door.

By sunrise, Dulcie had had enough. She got up and looked out the window. The police car was still there. The house was silent. She shoved the bureau away from the door, trying to be as quiet as possible, then clicked the lock on the doorknob. Cautiously, she opened the door and peeked out.

The first thing that she saw was Isabel's room across the hall. The door was open. *'Odd,'* thought Dulcie. *'She isn't an early riser. Maybe all the sleep she's been getting has thrown her off schedule?'* Dulcie quietly stepped into the hallway and looked in the room.

The bed was made. Everything was in place as it had been. But what slowly dawned on Dulcie was that none of Isabel's things were in the room. She quickly went in and looked in the closet, opened bureau drawers, even looked under the bed. Nothing. She went into the bathroom. Isabel's toilet kit was gone.

Dulcie rushed downstairs. She ran into the kitchen, and there she saw the note.

Dulcie,

Thank you for everything. I've been a terrible burden. I know you mean well, but I feel that I have put you in danger and I cannot allow that to happen. Please do not try to contact me. I need to disappear so that she can never find me again.

With kind regards,
Isabel

Dulcie grabbed her phone and at the same time flew out the door toward the police car. Tommy saw her coming and immediately elbowed his partner awake, then jumped out before she had even crossed the street. "What is it? What's happened?" he shouted.

"Did you see someone leave here? A woman? Small, dark hair…? Dulcie asked breathlessly as she reached him.

"Yes, about an hour ago. She left quietly and walked up the street. I thought she was a roommate or something going to work. There was no disturbance, so I didn't call in to the station…" Tommy looked worried. Now he thought he had done something wrong.

"No, it's fine. You had no need to call. You're right, there was not disturbance and I'm fine. It's okay." Dulcie scurried across the quiet street again as Tommy slowly got back into the car.

During the second ring Nick answered.

"She's run off again!" Dulcie exclaimed without letting him speak.

"What?"

"She left me a note! The policeman said she left about an hour ago!"

"Let me talk to him," Nick said.

Dulcie went back to the sidewalk and motioned to Tommy. He looked like a dog with its tail between its legs as he came across the street. Dulcie handed him the phone. "It's Detective Black," she said.

Now Tommy looked even worse. "Yes, sir?" Dulcie heard him say. As he listened, his back began to straighten. His eyes brightened. "Yes, sir! I'm on it, sir! Yes, I'll check back in with you in half an hour, sir!"

He handed the phone back and jumped in the car. His partner looked bewildered as they drove off.

"Wow, what did you tell him?" Dulcie asked Nick.

"He's doing concentric circles, keeping a lookout for her. I'll get others on it, too. Tommy's good at staying up all night, but he's not the brightest bulb in the chandelier."

Dulcie suddenly realized that she was standing in the street wearing her pajamas. She hurried back inside. "What else do you need from me?" she said.

"I need to see that note. I'll be there in fifteen minutes," he replied.

"Okay, the coffee will be ready." Dulcie put down the phone and looked down at herself. *'No time for a shower. But I need to get cleaned up at least!'* she thought. She groaned thinking of how ridiculous she was being. Twenty minutes before she had been in fear for her life. Now she was worried about how she would look when Nick came over. "Funny how our priorities change so quickly," she said out loud while scooping coffee into the machine and filling it with water. She hit the brew button and raced upstairs.

Hair brushed, teeth brushed, jeans and a polo shirt on in record time, she zipped down the stairs again just as Nick knocked on the door. As he came in, she could smell the soap that he used. *'Must have just jumped out of the shower,'* she thought. *'Men can do that. It isn't fair.'* She gestured toward the coffee maker. "Help yourself," she said and handed him Isabel's note.

Nick glanced at his watch. Quarter past six. "I have to call the doctor that signed off on the autopsy. We need another test done." He went into the other room and Dulcie heard him talking on the phone.

He had not even stopped for the coffee. She poured two cups, then joined him in the living room and handed him one. He looked at her gratefully while still talking. She heard him asking about quinine.

When the conversation ended he took a large gulp of coffee, winced at how hot it was, then read the note. "It doesn't really tell us anything," he said. "She could really be frightened, or she could have gone somewhere to meet up with Linda. I put a surveillance team on Linda's place after I talked with you last night. And I left a message with the doctor, but he needed me to call back with more information. This could get really interesting."

Dulcie nodded. "As far as I'm concerned, we passed *'interesting'* a long time ago!" she said.

"Can you show me the sections in Linda's notebook where you found those things you told me about last night?"

Dulcie nodded. She put down her coffee and turned to her desk. Then she remembered that her laptop was upstairs in the bedroom. "Oh, hang on a second. I brought it upstairs last night. I was paranoid that Isabel might get up, look at it, and see what I was up to."

"Rightly so," Nick said.

Dulcie hurried up the stairs. She tripped on a step and smacked her shin. Choking back a yelp and hoping Nick hadn't noticed, she kept going. As she came back down she tried not to limp. She opened the laptop and handed it to him.

"You okay?" he said without looking up at her. "You'll have a bruise for sure."

Dulcie felt her face turning red. "Yes, I'm okay and yes, I will."

"I know you haven't had much sleep." This time he did look at her with concern in his eyes. "Sorry you're part of all this. Once again."

Why did she feel as though she was melting every time he looked at her like that? It was really getting to be annoying. She tried to appear businesslike. "Here's the reference to the leg cramp medication," she said pointing to the computer screen. She reached over the keyboard, brushing his hand. Paging back through the images she stopped at one and said, "Here are those airport codes."

Nick nodded. "What made you think about quinine?"

"I don't really know. It was several things. I was curious about what she might take for leg cramps.

Then I found out that quinine is still prescribed in the UK. That made me think of the old remedies for things, from centuries ago, which made me think of quinine as a cure for malaria, then as an ingredient in most tonic water." Dulcie stopped, looking a bit confused. "My mind kind of went in a few directions."

"Well, we still don't know for certain, but it's worth checking." Nick's phone rang. "It's the coroner," he said looking at the number. He answered, then listened intently. "I'm not buying it. I think she forged the signature. ... No, unfortunately I can't get proof at the moment. The wife ran off. Again. ... She's there? Now? She just showed up now? You're sure it's Dumbarton's wife? Make sure she stay's put – get security on them please! I'll be right down."

Nick tossed back the rest of his coffee and handed the cup to Dulcie. "Found Isabel. She's at the morgue. Evidently she signed off on the cremation. I have to get over there, now!"

"Wait! Can I come? I might be able to help with Isabel. She trusts me."

"Good idea. Come on!"

They raced out of the house and jumped in Nick's car. As he drove, Dulcie began speculating. "Maybe Isabel just wants to be done with all of this and go home. Maybe Linda intimidated her. Maybe she's in league with Linda. Maybe..."

They finally reached the morgue. Dulcie had never been in one before. She expected to see bodies lying out on tables. Instead, she stood in a waiting room that looked like any other doctor's office. "Stay here for a minute, okay?" Nick said. It wasn't a question.

Nick went through a door opposite the entrance. Dulcie waited. She heard nothing. She sat down. Grabbing a magazine, she flipped through without seeing any of the pages. She stood and began pacing the room.

At last the door opened. Isabel came through with Nick. "What's happening?" said Dulcie.

"The doctor will be doing one last test to check for quinine in his system," Nick said simply.

"I know Linda had a prescription for it," said Isabel. "I saw it with her things. When I asked her about it, she said that she had leg cramps, but I had never heard her complain of them before." Isabel sat down heavily. She looked as though she had aged by twenty years in the past several days. "Detective Black just explained what quinine is. The doctor showed me a list of side effects. Confusion. Blurred vision. Heart problems. Logan seemed to experience all of these." She looked up at both of them. "I believe he was poisoned. She poisoned him. But why? She knew his will had been changed. Why would she want to kill him?"

They exchanged looks. No one had the answer.

Suddenly, Nick remembered. The storage facility. Her earlier trip to Portland. Bryce's report that he had seen her at the gallery. He turned to Isabel. "How many paintings did Logan typically complete in a year?"

She tipped her head sideways, thinking. "Complete? Perhaps three, at the most."

Nick shook his head. "That doesn't fit. Would he have any older works lying around that weren't in galleries?"

"No, Linda made sure that all of his completed works were hung as soon as possible," Isabel replied.

Dulcie realized what Nick was getting at. She had also remembered the storage company written in Linda's notebook. "Isabel, how many works did Logan typically start, but not complete?"

Now Isabel laughed. "I often teased him about that. I think he would start at least one a week, but usually would cast them aside. I never understood why he did not complete them. They always looked lovely to me, even as they were. He had dozens in his studio in London."

Dulcie heard Nick's sharp intake of breath. He quickly pulled out his phone. "Johnson," he said. "Get a team over to Holden's Holdings. The sister may be there. I think she has a stash of Dumbarton's paintings. Keep her there." He paused for a moment, listening, then said, "Yeah, I just talked to Dr. Kraus. They're having another look at the body," he glanced over at Isabel, "Uh, I mean, Dumbarton."

He toyed with the phone after the call ended, trying to decide what to do next. "I think you two should go home. Get some rest. This could take a while," he finally said.

Dulcie eyed him pointedly. "Could I speak to you for a moment?" she nearly barked. "I'm sorry Isabel, excuse us please." Dulcie pulled Nick into the hallway. "What the hell are you doing? Last night you insight terror, implying that Isabel might want to kill me, and now you tell me to bring her home again? Alone?"

She was right, of course, but Nick trusted his instincts. He had been concerned the night before, but now he realized that Isabel had no part in any of it. It was entirely Linda's doing. If only the quinine tests were positive, he would have her. "Look, Dulcie. I know I'm being unreasonable. Please just trust me. This is all Linda. Isabel is innocent. I'm sure of it. Please, trust me."

'Why?' thought Dulcie, *'because you've proven yourself to be worthy of it? I hardly think so.'* Her saner half relented, however. The more she thought about the events since

Logan's death, the more she agreed with him. "Fine," she said at last.

She looked like an insolent child. Nick nearly laughed, but felt more sympathy for her than anything else. Most likely she was exhausted, not to mention completely confused. "I'll take you guys home," he said.

The drive was very quiet. When they reached Dulcie's house she realized how tired she was. "Isabel, I have to get some sleep. Do you mind?"

"I was thinking the same thing," she said. "He will call us?" she asked, motioning toward Nick's car as he drove away.

"He will," Dulcie replied. She went into her room and closed the door. She heard Isabel go into the guest room. Dulcie waited several moments, then she locked the door as quietly as possible and pulled the bureau in front of it. *'No sense taking chances,'* she thought.

Dulcie heard a buzzing sound in the distance. She was groggy. Somewhere in the haze she thought a bee was in her pocket. Then the mist in her mind began to clear. It was her phone.

She yanked it out and glanced at the time. Nearly noon. The phone had stopped ringing. While she stared at it, the voicemail signal popped on. She pressed it.

Nick. "Dulcie, call me. It isn't good news."

She quickly hit the Return Call button. "What happened?" she asked.

"Inconclusive. They found quinine, and it was more than he'd have from a few tonic waters, but they can't conclude that it brought about his heart failure."

"Well, what else could have caused it? Seriously, he didn't have a heart condition. Do people suddenly drop from heart failure? I don't think so," Dulcie said, exasperated.

"Uh, actually they do," Nick said quietly. "But that's irrelevant. I've had a crew over at the storage place all morning, but Linda hasn't gone there yet. We don't know where she is. Dammit, I *know* she killed him!"

"You just can't prove it." Dulcie stated the obvious. "Sorry, I guess you knew that already."

"That's okay. I know you're frustrated too. At this point, without a confession, I can't do anything."

'*A confession!*' thought Dulcie. "Nick, I have to go. Keep me posted."

"Yeah," he grunted.

Dulcie began pacing the room. '*It has to be Isabel,*' she thought. Isabel was the only one who could pull out the details. She would have to provoke Linda somehow. Isabel would have to make her angry. It would be the only way to make Linda say anything.

Dulcie shoved the bureau away from the door. '*I have to stop doing this,*' she thought. She yanked at the doorknob before realizing that she had locked the door. "And now I'm losing my mind," she said out loud.

As she thumped down the stairs she heard Isabel rummaging in the kitchen. She looked up as Dulcie came in. "It isn't exactly tea time, but I've made some anyway. Would you like a cup?"

"Isabel, you have no idea. Absolutely!" It was then that she noticed Isabel was pouring from a beautifully painted ceramic teapot. "Is that yours?" she asked.

"No," Isabel said. "It's yours. You didn't have one, and I thought you should. It's my *thank you* for making me feel safe here. I slipped out about an hour ago and got it at the shop down the street."

Dulcie instantly felt like an idiot for barricading her bedroom door. She knew that the *'shop down the street'* was an expensive antiques store. "Well, thank you for such a beautiful gift. I'm glad I could help, although you shouldn't have gone out."

"Yes, but that nice bobby was across the street. His partner walked down with me, and even carried it back. They were quite lovely toward me." She sipped her tea.

'Good looks and charm,' thought Dulcie. *'That's all it takes.'* However, she realized that what she really needed to ask of Isabel was going to require a lot more than simply good looks or charm. "Isabel, I've just spoken with Nick. There's a problem."

Isabel's dark eyes widened but she said nothing.

Dulcie continued. "The tests on Logan did show quinine but they can't determine if that's what killed him. At this point, the police have nothing on Linda."

Isabel shook her head so fiercely that her tea spilled from her cup. "No! They have to! I know she did it. I know she killed him!"

"But, why Isabel? Why would she?"

"There are so many possible reasons, I can't say for sure." She looked up at Dulcie pointedly. "I know what you're thinking," she said, "and you're right. I have to talk to her. I'm the only one that could make her confess."

Dulcie nodded. It was exactly what she was about to ask Isabel to do.

"I'll do it. I'm scared, but I'll do it. She can't get away with this. It's the least I can do for Logan, after tricking him in the first place. It won't take away my guilt, but I'll know I did the right thing in the end."

Dulcie agreed. Then she realized how hungry she was. She reached into the refrigerator and found the rest of her fried rice. "Want some?" she asked Isabel.

"I'm famished!" she replied.

Dulcie pulled out two forks. She was about to dish the rice into bowls and put them in the microwave, but Isabel grabbed the carton from her. "Never mind that!" she said and dug her fork in. Dulcie laughed and did the same.

C3

They leaned against the cold, metal folding door of the large storage locker opposite Linda's. Nick, Adam Johnson, Dulcie, and Isabel along with several uniformed officers had been waiting for an hour. "What if she doesn't come?" asked Dulcie.

"She'll be here," Isabel said. "I know her. This is next on her list."

Johnson's phone buzzed. He looked at the text message that had come through. "She just drove in," he said. "Let's move."

They scattered to their positions. Isabel flattened herself into a niche made by the locker just beyond Linda's. She waited, holding her breath, hoping that Linda wouldn't see her. She wanted to check her microphone to make sure that it was still on, but didn't dare. Nick had said it was fine, but Isabel knew she had only one chance.

Hidden behind a stack of cardboard boxes, Dulcie could not see Isabel but she had an excellent view of the door of Linda's locker. She strained to hear if someone was coming. At last, footsteps, muffled on the cement floor. She heard a squeaking sound, like a wheel. When Linda came into view, Dulcie saw that she was pulling a dolly behind her. Linda stopped in front of her locker and pulled out a key. She leaned over and unlocked the metal door, then heaved it up on its tracks. The locker was like a garage for a very small car.

Linda switched on a light. Dulcie saw boxes. They looked like substantial crates used for shipping. Linda rolled the dolly into the locker and slid it under one of the boxes. Dulcie saw her lift a second box and was surprised at her strength. They looked heavy. As she turned to put it on top of the other, Isabel stepped into the doorway.

"My goodness, what have we here?" she said with mock sincerity.

Linda froze. Isabel took several steps into the locker, careful to keep at least one box between herself and Linda as Detective Black had instructed her.

"No, don't tell me. Let me guess. Charity for the poor? No, that wouldn't be it. You've never been philanthropic. Hmmmm. Let me see. I know! You're moving to America! No, that won't do either. You've always said that you dislike the Yanks. Hmm." She tapped her chin with a finger. "I've got it! You killed your brother, and now you're going to sell all of his paintings here and run off with the money!" She tilted her head and smiled. "Linda, that's brilliant! Except for one tiny flaw. You never informed me." She stopped. And waited.

Linda was still silent. *'Damn!'* thought Isabel. *'I have to get her talking! Why won't she say anything?'*

"That's fine, Linda. At least I know now. The trouble for you is that I have everything else. And now,

I know everything else." she glared at her sister-in-law, and said very quietly, "So you see, I'm in charge now."

Linda sneered. "You could never be in charge, you stupid bitch! All you did was wreck my plans. Our plans."

"The plan did not include killing my husband."

"He was your *husband* in name only! Besides, you were getting too close. I couldn't let you start caring for him. That's all I needed – to have him in my life for another thirty or forty years! He had to go."

"You *knew* he was an alcoholic. You were the one who kept him sober for years! You *knew* he wouldn't be able to resist those gin and tonics. That's how you did it, wasn't it! He didn't die of a heart attack! Not without your help, anyway!" Isabel shouted.

"I thought you and I would be together! I thought you cared about me! We had plans!" shrieked Linda. "My only regret now is that I didn't take you out, too!"

The box moved so fast and hit her with such force that it knocked Isabel backwards out of the locker. She slammed against the metal door on the opposite side. She saw Linda hoisting another box, poised to throw it at her. Isabel screamed.

At the last moment, three uniformed police jumped forward and grabbed Linda.

Isabel slid to the floor. Her heart was pounding. Dulcie ran to her. "I'm fine," Isabel said. "Just a few bruises." She winced as she tried to move, but then smiled up at Dulcie. "That was actually quite exciting!"

Nick had been giving orders to the officers who were now putting handcuffs on Linda. He came over to Dulcie and Isabel. "Don't move," he said to Isabel. "I've got paramedics coming. I just want to make sure nothing is broken.

Isabel nodded, then winced again. "Even if something is, it was worth it!" she said. "Did you hear everything?"

"Loud and clear," Nick said. "Loud and clear."

I don't say everything,
but I paint everything.
~ Pablo Picasso

CHAPTER ELEVEN

The students of Logan Dumbarton's Master Class in Abstract Painting sat in the studio of the Maine Museum of Art. Two weeks before, their easels had been set up, their brushes and paints ready, and they had all eagerly anticipated the arrival of the great artist himself.

Today, they sat quietly with none of their materials. "Why are we here?" Mary finally whispered loudly. Everyone heard her. Her sister laughed nervously. "Do they think one of us killed Logan?"

Kimberly was the only one who had any inkling that Tara might be correct. She did have a hunch that it wasn't one of them, however.

Dulcie came in to the room, followed by Detective Black and Isabel Dumbarton. Isabel's left arm was in a sling.

"Hi everyone." Dulcie said. "Looks like a nice day to paint. Too bad we aren't outside." It was an attempt at humor. No one laughed.

"I guess I'll get right down to business. I want to apologize to all of you for the way this class turned out. I think that the words *complete and utter failure* might describe it best. I have checks here for all of you to refund the tuition in full."

Bethany leaned forward. She was a different Bethany than the one everybody had seen before. She wore faded jeans, a bright orange peasant blouse, and silver hoop earrings. Her hair had been tinted with blonde highlights and it now had soft waves. "I for one can't agree with your description of this class. For me, I'd call it a complete success." She didn't elaborate. She didn't have to.

"I'd have to agree with Bethany," said Bryce. "I did get quite a bit out of it." He glanced over at Willow who smiled and looked away quickly. "But I'll take the check anyway." They all laughed.

"That's fine," Dulcie said. "And along with reimbursement, I think we also owe you an explanation." She glanced at Nick. He nodded.

"Evidently, we were all pawns in a game that had been carefully constructed some time ago. I was the biggest dupe, however." They looked at her curiously. "It seems that Linda Dumbarton was getting tired of living in the shadows and managing her brother's career. She engineered the entire trip to Maine along with this class. It had been her suggestion from the start." Dulcie paused. She had already decided not to mention Isabel's relationship with Linda. It wasn't necessary. Isabel would only come across as manipulative, at best.

"Logan Dumbarton started many paintings, but finished very few. He was very critical of his own work."

"Not as critical as he was of ours," Scott said.

"That's probably true," replied Dulcie, "But the point is that he had many unfinished canvases that he abandoned in his gallery. Unfinished in his eyes, that is. To anyone else, they looked very complete. At some point, Linda realized this. She practiced signing his name exactly as he did. Then she began collecting them.

"Linda took her time slipping them out of the studio. She boxed up only a few at a time. Then, she shipped them to Portland, where she arranged for them to be stored until she arrived. Her plan was to sell them in art galleries in the US."

"So I was right! I knew I had seen her!" Bryce said. He looked around at the others. "She came to the gallery where I work a few months ago. I didn't realize it at first. Took me forever to place her when I saw her again at the class."

Dulcie continued. "Linda didn't realize that, although Portland is a city, Maine is a small place. It's hard to hide here. You're bound to be noticed, eventually.

Isabel stepped forward. "Could I tell them the next bit?" she asked in her soft British accent. Both Dulcie and Nick nodded. "I hadn't known Logan for long before we married. I didn't know his secrets. One of them was that he was an alcoholic. It was something that he kept to himself. Linda knew this, however. Shortly after our marriage, Linda began suggesting drinks to him. I didn't think anything of it. But when he drank, he couldn't stop. That wasn't the worst of it, though. When he drank, he was also mean, rude, snide, bitter... everything that all of you were unfortunate enough to encounter. And for that I apologize."

"No apology needed," said Kimberly warmly. "You clearly did all you could to alleviate the situation." Heads bobbed up and down in agreement.

"Linda suggested that we come to America. I hoped that it would be the interlude that we needed to get Logan to stop drinking. It wasn't," she added simply. "I became desperate. The night before he died, I put turpentine in his drink. It smelled like gin, so I thought that he wouldn't notice, especially after he'd had several. I just wanted to make him sick, and hopefully that would keep him from drinking them any more." She stopped, looked at the floor and swallowed hard several times.

Nick cleared his throat. "Isabel thought she had poisoned Logan and killed him. She had not. His official cause of death was heart failure. It would have been an open and shut case, except that other facts were still there that didn't seem to make sense. For example, Linda had lied on several occasions, but the lies seemed trivial and unnecessary. Our conclusion was that she was hiding something."

"So, no one killed Logan? He really died of a heart attack?" asked Tara.

"Yes... and no," answered Dulcie. "It seems that Linda was putting quinine in Logan's gin and tonics. You might know that quinine is already in tonic water, which helped to mask the bitter test of the extra amount. It's still prescribed in England for leg cramps, and Linda had it with her. One of the unfortunate side-effects of overdose is potential heart failure. Evidently the quinine can't be linked to Logan's heart attack conclusively, but at the very least, Linda attempted to murder him. Whether she succeeded or whether he simply died is for someone else to decide."

"So now that he's dead," Bryce began, then looked quickly at Isabel. "Oh, sorry, I don't mean any disrespect. But, now that he's gone, his paintings are worth a bundle!"

"That's what Linda was counting on, it seems," said Nick.

Everyone was silent for a moment. Dulcie stepped forward. "So, that appears to be the end of it," she said as she handed out envelopes to each of them. "Thanks to all of you for suffering through this, and for your patience. I don't think I'll be scheduling a master class again for quite some time, but I hope to see everyone in the museum. Please come by my office and say hello when you visit us next."

The students stood and, chatting with each other, slowly filtered out of the room. The only one remaining was Kimberly. "Coffee?" she said to Dulcie. "Do you have time?"

"Yes I do!" Dulcie answered. She had been trying to figure out a way to leave without having to speak with Nick again. He and Isabel were talking at the front of the room. "Isabel," she interrupted. "I'm going to get a coffee with Kimberly. Can you get back to the house okay? You have the key, right?"

Isabel nodded. "A walk in this nice, ocean air would be lovely. Then, a spot of tea, and I'll plan my trip home. I think you'll be glad to see the back of me," she said.

"Not at all. You've been a wonderful guest, in spite of your unfortunate choice in friends. Or spouse." Dulcie smirked. "I'll shut up now. See you later." Dulcie glanced at Nick as she left the room. "Thanks for all your help, Detective," she said bluntly.

A stunned look crossed Nick's face, but was replaced quickly by his more typical stoic expression.

Kimberly sipped her coffee while sitting in Dulcie's office. "It wasn't quite what I expected, but it was the most fun I've had in a long time!" she said. "Oh dear! I suppose I shouldn't say that. After all, that poor man did die!"

Dulcie chuckled and said, "I know exactly what you mean. It was a complete disaster, but at least Isabel escaped from a very bad situation."

Kimberly gave Dulcie a sideways glance. "Is there perhaps more to that story than I know, or shouldn't I ask?"

Dulcie looked at the heavens for a moment then laughed. "All right! Yes, there's more. It may or may not come out."

"My lips are sealed," said Kimberly, sliding her fingers along them as though closing a zipper.

"It seems that the marriage was a front to begin with. Linda and Isabel were the couple, not Logan and Isabel."

"Was Logan aware of this?" asked Kimberly, her eyes wide. "And how did they pull that off, unless Isabel is…"

"Logan has been unable to, um, carry out the duties of a husband, shall we say, for years. He was simply infatuated with Isabel and wanted her as a companion. She and Linda initially thought it was a fine arrangement, but Isabel began feeling guilty once she realized that Logan was in love with her, and Linda was increasingly jealous."

"Ah yes," Kimberly sighed. "The old love triangle rears it's ugly head. Add greed and anger, stir, and you've got a recipe for disaster. But I am glad that

Isabel was able to come out of it all right. I think that deep down, she has a good heart."

"I think you're right," Dulcie said.

"Speaking of hearts, you know that policeman is in love with you."

Kimberly's words shocked Dulcie. She swallowed wrong and began coughing. "What?" was all she could manage to squawk.

Kimberly just shook her head and smiled. "It's so obvious. It's the way he looks at you. I must say, he does seem very nice. And you could do a lot worse in the looks department," she giggled with a soft, bubbling sound. Then she put down her empty coffee cup and waved her hand as if brushing away the topic. "As I say, though, this is the most fun I've had in a long time. I have you to thank for that!"

Dulcie had recovered. "Kimberly, I hope I've gained a new friend. Please come by again?" Dulcie put out her hand to shake Kimberly's.

Kimberly stood and took Dulcie's hand in both of hers. She pressed it warmly. "I'm actually considering becoming a volunteer docent, so you may see a lot more of me, whether you like it or not!" She winked at Dulcie as she left.

ೞ

Several days later, Nick drove his eight-year-old ugly blue Honda north out of Boston. He was a free man. Everything had cleared the courts, the papers had been signed, and it was over. She had not appeared, of course. Her lawyers were there instead. Initially he had been disappointed. One final showdown might have been nice, to tell her exactly how he felt. On the other hand, maybe it was for the best. He had won. It was a slow, painful battle, but he had won.

Nick's birthday was in one week. He would be thirty. A new chapter of a new life. His lawyer had explained the transfer of the trust fund to him. It was something that no one in his family could block, the legacy of his grandparents. Nick thought about them. Although his grandfather had begun the law firm that Nick had been groomed to join, somehow Nick knew that he would have understood why Nick needed to take a different path. After all, isn't that exactly what his grandfather had done? His father, Nick's great-grandfather, had been a successful restaurateur, who sold the business he had so carefully constructed when no one in the family wanted to take it over. He had given the money to his son, his only child, to start his own law business. Yes, his grandfather would have certainly understood.

Nick had already decided that the money would change very little in his life. He would invest most of it. True, he might get a new car. He chuckled thinking that this current wreck had seen better days. The new one would still be practical, though. Nothing flashy. Well, maybe just a little flashy.

Nick drove steadily on in the silence. He liked the silence. He could think.

His thoughts drifted to Dulcie. He found them doing this frequently as of late. He knew that she didn't trust him. He knew that he should have told her from the start about his background. It was stupid to keep it a secret, really. It had been a defense mechanism, a way from feeling the pain himself. He knew that now, and hoped it wasn't too late.

03

Dulcie sat on the deck of her brother's yacht, sipping a glass of wine as the boat gently moved up and down with the waves. Dan emerged from the cabin. "Jeez, Dulcie, you're getting to be quite an old hand at this murder thing. I'm actually kind of scared to be around you now. I mean, what if I'm next?" He sat down on the bench opposite her.

"Sorry, Dan. No such luck. They couldn't even prove this last one was murder. Everyone is pretty certain it was, but they can only go with attempted murder this time, or so I've heard." She glanced over at him with a sly smile. "So at least that gives you a fighting chance!"

"That's all I need to get the hell out," he muttered. "Of course it did throw you back in with loverboy there."

"Will you cut it out?" Dulcie huffed. "Yes, I had to work with him again. But it's done. It's over."

Dan gave her an incredulous look. Dulcie huffed again. Dan tossed back the rest of his beer and spun around sideways on the bench. "Long day today. Wake me up in half an hour?" He settled back into the cushions. His eyes were closed already.

Dulcie felt her cell phone vibrate. She forgot that it was still in silent mode. She pulled it out. "Call from NICK" it read. She froze. The phone kept vibrating.

"You gonna answer that?" Dan said, eyes still closed.

Dulcie glanced over at him, then back at the phone. "I don't know," she said. "I really don't know."

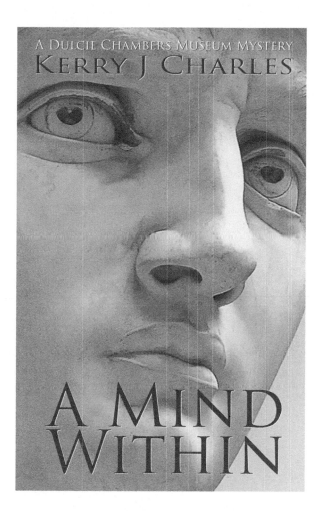

A Dulcie Chambers Museum Mystery

KERRY J CHARLES

A MIND WITHIN

THE DULCIE CHAMBERS
MUSEUM MYSTERIES

Book #4:

A MIND WITHIN

CHAPTER 1

It wasn't a face. He never saw a face. It was only curves and lines and colors that seemed to move around each other and grow, from the top of the canvas down to the bottom. It never started with an oval, then eyes, perhaps a mouth next, the tricky nose placed in between, as artists throughout the millennia had painted portraits. His always began at the top and worked its way down. It wasn't a face. Not to him.

Dulcie watched in amazement. He began with one swooping stroke. A lock of brown hair starting at the top, sliding half way down the canvas. Then another, and another. Then eyebrows... eyes beneath. A nose... ears... mouth. Chin, neck, shoulders.... Each was perfectly rendered before he moved on to the next.

She had entered the room only ten minutes before and he had barely glanced at her, yet it was as though she was looking into a mirror. He had captured her likeness so perfectly, so exactly. How was it possible?

"Has he seen me before?" Dulcie asked without taking her eyes off his work. The woman beside her shrugged her shoulders.

"Possibly. He has been to the art museum. He might have seen you in a newspaper article as well. Perhaps." She had a soft accent. French, or possibly French-Canadian.

The young man abruptly put down his brush and walked to the window. He was done.

"What now?" asked Dulcie quietly.

"Now it goes in the stack with the others," the woman gestured toward the corner of the room. Dozens of paintings were propped against the wall, mostly portraits, from what Dulcie could see. Many looked as though they were of the same person: a middle-aged man. "Unless you want it?" the woman asked Dulcie.

"May I?"

The woman shrugged again.

"I feel as though I should ask him," Dulcie said.

"You can try, but I'm afraid you won't get a response," the woman replied. It was not said unkindly, simply as a matter of fact.

Dulcie crossed the room and stood beside the young man. She knew that he was fifteen. She didn't look at him, she simply stood beside him and looked out the window as he did. He was still, silent. At last Dulcie said softly, "May I have the painting of me?"

Nothing. Then, in one slow gesture, he turned his hand and opened it so that the palm faced up.

"Thank you," Dulcie whispered.

The other woman in the room had not noticed. She was attending to her work, making sure that the room was in order, that the young man would have what he needed. Dulcie couldn't know that his simple gesture was the first communication that he had made in months.

ↄ৪

"What the heck is that?" Dulcie's brother exclaimed as he entered Dulcie's office in the Maine Museum of Art. He pointed to an odd assemblage of bottle caps. Thousands of them were stuck together, forming a human-sized Statue of Liberty.

Dan Chambers never minced words, which made Dulcie laugh. However, she knew his reaction would be common among visitors viewing the new exhibit.

"It's called Outsider Art," she said.

"Never heard of it."

"I wouldn't imagine that you had," she said. "Most people haven't. It comes from the French *art brut* which means raw or rough art. It can mean a lot of things, but it includes art made by people who aren't professional artists, such as indigents, people with brain traumas, the insane... even children. Basically, they're compelled to create, usually beyond a level that we would consider normal."

"Wow," Dan simply stated. He hadn't taken his eyes of the statue. "What's it stuck together with?" he asked, leaning in for a closer look.

"Gum," Dulcie said.

"You mean like gummy glue kind of stuff?"

"No, I mean chewing gum," she replied.

Dan instantly pulled back. "Gross!"

Dulcie shook her head. "Well, it's completely hardened by now, silly. The thing is at least five years old. The police found it in an abandoned warehouse outside of Boston. They knew there was a homeless guy living there for a while. They didn't bother him since he never caused any trouble, they said, but they had no idea he was making this," she nodded toward the statue. "When he died on the streets, they went to the place where they knew he'd been staying and found the statue."

Dan was more appreciative standing a few feet back. "I wonder how long it took him to make?"

"Good question! I have so many questions about it, which we'll never have answers for, unfortunately."

Dan crossed the room and sat in the chair by his sister's desk. He was still amazed that she was the director of the entire museum. She definitely had the brains in the family, although he had his own kind of common-sense wisdom. "So is this the beginnings of a new exhibit?" he asked.

"Yes, and I'm pretty excited about it. I'm hoping that it will get people thinking about what really defines art. We always assume it's Leonardos and such. But it's much more basic to the human psyche than that. It's expression and communication, and probably a lot of other things."

"Thank you for the lecture, Dr. Chambers," Dan said with mock applause.

She smirked at him. "Someone needs to broaden your horizons," she said looking back at her computer. "I've got a lot of pieces coming in over the next couple of days," she said, scrolling through images. "It's gonna get busy."

Dulcie stood up quickly, making her brother jump. "Hey," she said, "come down to my car. I want to show you something."

They left her office, walking by the museum's front desk. Dan winked at Dulcie's assistant, Rachel. She giggled. Dulcie rolled her eyes at her brother. "Stop that!" she mouthed.

In the parking lot, Dulcie opened the back of her ancient Jeep Wrangler. She had known for some time that she should get a new vehicle, but couldn't bear to part with it. Not yet.

"What do you think of this?" she asked, pulling out the portrait of herself.

"*Aaahhhh!*" Dan yelled in fear, putting his hand over his heart in mock terror at the sight. Dulcie swatted him. "Sorry. Had to," he grinned. "But seriously, it's definitely you. When did you sit for a portrait?"

"That's the weird thing. I didn't. This is another example of Outsider Art. A young man, actually more like a kid – he's only 15 – painted this of me today. He barely even glanced at me, and I was standing behind him when he made it."

Dan shook his head in disbelief. "How is that even possible?"

"Yeah, I agree. He's an autistic savant. He paints and draws for hours every day but hasn't spoken, ever. Not that anyone knows about, anyway."

"Huh! I'd never be able to pull that off," Dan said. "The speaking bit, I mean." He looked back at the painting. "Or this either, come to think of it."

Dulcie glanced over at her brother and laughed. He was such an extrovert. She couldn't imagine him *not* speaking. She closed the car door, carefully holding the painting away. "All right, back to work," she said.

"Yeah," Dan sighed. I've gotta go scrub down the boat. I hate that chore, but has to be done or it'll look terrible inside of a week." He gave his sister a wave and headed off in the direction of the waterfront.

Dan ran his own business, taking people on tours around Portland Harbor and Casco Bay in his small private yacht. Dulcie was his silent partner, and had invested an unexpected inheritance in his business to buy the boat. Dan lived on board and, with his natural storytelling abilities and ease with people, had made the business thrive.

Dulcie watched him walk away knowing that his momentary dejection would quickly pass. He loved everything about that boat. She clicked the lock on the door of the Jeep, noticing yet another scratch in the paint. Bringing the painting inside, she carefully set it on a table in her office, tipping it against the wall behind. She stood back and cocked her head sideways as she gazed at it. Xander Bellamy. She had heard of him, but it was the first time that she had met him.

Rachel knocked on the doorframe of Dulcie's office and walked in. She stopped immediately when she saw the painting. "That's awesome!" she said. "When'd you get that done? And why?" Her eyes grew big as she realized she'd just made a faux pas. "I mean, not 'why' exactly. But, it doesn't seem like something you'd do. Have a portrait made. Of yourself. Not that there's anything wrong with doing that," she was stammering now.

Dulcie turned and grinned at her assistant. "Easy, Rachel! No offence taken," she laughed. "I know what you're getting at. I'm not exactly the type for self-aggrandizement. I'd rather fade into the woodwork, given the choice." She looked over at the painting.

"But this has kind of a weird story behind it. Have you heard of Xander Bellamy?"

Rachel thought for a moment. Her clear blue eyes squinted. "I know that name," she said slowly. Then she snapped her fingers. "He's the guy that was in the news a few months ago, right? Didn't his father kill his grandfather or something like that?"

Dulcie nodded. "Yes, and it was pretty sad. I just looked up the story. His mother had died several years ago, too. He's autistic and doesn't speak. His father was devoted to him but I guess the grandfather didn't have much to do with them, even though they all lived in the same house."

"Was he the father's father or the mother's? The grandfather, I mean," asked Rachel. She always tried to get the details straight, a trait that Dulcie loved since it helped with her work enormously.

"The mother's father."

"And didn't he fall off a balcony or out of a window or something like that?" asked Rachel.

"Yes, and there was some speculation that he was pushed by Xander although no one could imagine why. But then the father stepped forward and confessed that he had pushed him. They had been arguing, he said. It was all very strange and tragic."

"Sounds it," replied Rachel. "So how does Xander fit in with this?" she pointed to the painting.

"He did it," Dulcie said simply.

Rachel's eyes were wide. "*Really?*"

"Yup. And furthermore, he did it after barely looking at me, plus it only took him a few minutes. I've never seen anything like it. He started at the top, worked his way to the bottom, and never went back to change or touch-up anything. Just put down his brush and walked away when he was done."

"But how did he have the colors? Didn't he need to mix them?"

"He had a lot of paint on his palette already. The woman that takes care of him said that he's been doing a lot of portraits lately. I saw a whole bunch in his studio that looked like they were all of the same person. He just used the paint he already had to do my portrait."

"Did you ask him to? Why did he paint you?"

"I have no idea," said Dulcie. She hadn't thought about that. Why had he chosen to paint her? "Very good question. I have no idea," she repeated quietly.

"Well, that's a mystery for another time," said Rachel, adopting her businesslike voice. "Right now, we've got some logistics to figure out. You've got four more artists for the new exhibit with two or three works each, and then three more with single works, right?"

Dulcie took a deep breath and shifted gears mentally. "Yes," she nodded at the list Rachel was holding. "Could you do the usual with shipping and insurance and such? Do you have everyone's contact info?"

Rachel nodded, her curly hair bouncing. "No problem." She turned to Dulcie's portrait again. "Are you going to include this?" she asked. "That qualifies as Outsider Art, I'd think."

"It certainly does, but there is no way I'm putting a portrait of me in the gallery!" Dulcie saw Rachel trying to hide a smile. "So don't even think about it!" Dulcie added. "But I do plan on exhibiting some of his work. It's too incredible not to." She sat back in her chair. "The difficult part about this exhibit is that every piece has a different story about the artist that made it.

I'll have to figure out a way to tell each story as briefly as possible."

"And tactfully, in some cases," Rachel added. "Anything else you need from me for now?" she asked.

Dulcie thought for a moment. "Nope. I think we're good for now, thanks."

Rachel was already heading for the door, her untamable hair bobbing up and down and her quick mind eager to take on the next project. Dulcie noticed she gave the bottle-cap-chewing-gum Statue of Liberty a wide berth.

ॐ

Adam Johnson wandered through the wine shop following his Portland Police Department partner and fellow detective, Nicholas Black, closely. Johnson tried to suck in his large stomach as much as possible and keep his arms pinned to his sides. He leaned over, ever so slightly, from time to time so that he could see an interesting looking label. A particular one caught his eye, and he gingerly picked it up. The label looked old, with ornate lettering.

"Pie-Not... pie-not NO-wer," he whispered to himself.

"Pinot Noir," Nick pronounced correctly over his shoulder.

"Pee-no newarr?" That sounds even worse!" Johnson said, aghast.

"It's a kind of grape," said Nick with a tinge of annoyance.

"Hmm," muttered Johnson, carefully replacing the bottle on the shelf. He shuffled behind Nick again as he moved to the next aisle.

Nick turned to face him. "Don't you have anything to do? You've been following me around for half the day now. I'm on lunch break, you know."

Johnson stared at the floor and stuffed his hands in his pockets. "Yeah, I know." He looked dejected.

Nick would have laughed but he knew his partner, Detective Adam Johnson, was serious. This really wasn't like him. "Hey," Nick said, "What's up?"

Johnson shook his head slowly, still looking down. "I'm in trouble," he said simply.

Now Nick was really concerned. Jovial, laid-back, devil-may-care Johnson was never in any trouble that he couldn't see himself out of within a very brief period of time. "Seriously? What sort of trouble?" Now that Nick thought about it, he hadn't even seen Johnson eating, which was a sure sign that something was wrong.

"It's this bet I have," Johnson began.

Nick's heart sank. Gambling? He would never have pegged Johnson as a gambler. Nick said quietly, "Do you need money, Adam?" Nick never called his partner by his first name, but the situation seemed so grave, he thought it was the right thing to say.

Johnson's head popped up again. "Well, now that you mention it…," he had a tiny twinkle in his eye, but it disappeared as he became lost in thought again.

"Okay, out with it!" Nick ordered.

Johnson sighed. "Fine. You'll find out soon enough. I've got a bet with the wife."

Nick relaxed with relief. At least it wasn't money. Or not serious money, at any rate. "And?" he said.

"And I'm losing."

"So what's the bet?"

Johnson shook his head with dismay again. "All right, here's the whole story. She made me go to the doctor for my snoring. She said it's like a freight train and she can't sleep. I bought her earplugs, but let's just say that that didn't go over well. So, I went to the doctor. He said I have sleep apnea. And high blood pressure. And I needed to lose weight. Otherwise, I'll have to wear some contraption when I sleep in case I don't breathe enough, and I'll have to go on some kind of blood pressure medication."

The gravity of the situation was beginning to dawn on Nick. Johnson really loved his food. "So you're on a diet?" he asked, trying not to smile.

"Yeah, you could say that. Plus, the wife and I made a bet. See, that was my big mistake. She said that I couldn't lose ten pounds in a month. She even gave me a back-up. I can either lose the ten pounds, or I can walk 300,000 steps. She gave me this," he took a little device off his belt. "It's a pedometer. She writes down how many steps I do every night." Johnson replaced it on his belt. "So far it's been a week. I haven't lost a pound, and I've only walked 37,562," he glanced at the device, "No, make that 63, steps."

Nick was laughing now. "Do I dare ask what happens if you lose?"

Johnson looked at the floor again and shoved his hands in his pockets. He said something that Nick couldn't hear.

"What's that?"

Johnson straightened up, eyed his partner squarely, and said, "A week for both of us at the La Dolce Vita Spa and Weight Loss Center. The former would be for her, the latter for me."

Nick began laughing harder. Johnson's wife was an adorable, petite Italian woman who commanded his life outside of his work. Johnson loved every second of it and everything about her. She was devoted to him as well. Nick had never known there to be any strife between them. "Is Maria upset with you?" he asked.

"No," Johnson said almost mournfully. "I think she's secretly hoping that I'll lose so she can go!"

Nick realized that, like Maria, he also assumed that Johnson would lose. Now he wondered what his end of the bet was. "What do you get if you win?"

Johnson instantly perked up. He stood straighter and a smile spread across his face like a ray of sunshine. "A week in Florida to see the Red Sox in spring training every day, including VIP tickets! And she gets me beer and sausages whenever I want them!" Johnson looked giddy. He rattled out the words so fast that Nick could barely understand them.

It was a grave situation, indeed.

A thought occurred to Johnson. "Hey! How 'bout if you wear this for a little while!" He started to take the pedometer off his belt again.

"Oh, no! No way! I'm not going to help you cheat!"

"Oh, c'mon! Just through lunch! I don't think it works right on me anyway. It doesn't count my steps right! Watch!" He walked down the aisle counting, then came back. "Ok, I said before I'd done something-something-63, right? So I just did fifteen steps It should be 78 now, right?" He looked down at the device, then back up at Nick. "Oh. It says 78. Okay, fine. It did work this time. But I swear…"

Nick shook his head and turned back to the wine selection. "Yeah, Johnson, I'd say you're in trouble. Right now, though, why don't you go outside and walk to the end of the block and back again. By the time you're at the door, I'll be done here. That should add maybe another hundred or so steps?"

Johnson sighed deeply and turned toward the door. "Yeah, okay. This place is kinda boring anyway."

If you would like to read more of A MIND WITHIN, please visit the author's web site (kerryjcharles.com) for more information, or request it at your local bookstore. Ebook versions are available from major suppliers online.

Reviews from thoughtful readers are always welcome on any website or media outlet. Thank you!

ABOUT THE AUTHOR

Kerry J Charles has worked as a researcher, writer, and editor for *National Geographic*, the Smithsonian Institution, Harvard University and several major textbook publishers. She holds four degrees including a Masters in Geospatial Engineering and a Masters in Art History from Harvard University. She has carried out research in many of the world's art museums as a freelance writer and scholar.

A swimmer, scuba diver, golfer, and boating enthusiast, Charles enjoys seeing the world from above and below sea level as well as from the tee box. Her life experiences inspire her writing and she is always seeking out new travels and adventures. She returned to her roots in coastal Maine while writing the Dulcie Chambers Museum Mysteries.

Made in the USA
Las Vegas, NV
27 November 2021